MERMAID OF MONTE CARLO

MERMAID OF VENICE: BOOK 6

JINCEY LUMPKIN

ABOUT THE AUTHOR

JINCEY LUMPKIN is a writer who splits her time between NYC and Lisbon. She has been profiled by Dateline NBC, *Vice*, and *GQ*, among others. *Out* Magazine listed her in its "OUT 100", naming her as one of the world's most influential LGBTQ+ people, alongside celebrities like Laverne Cox and Ricky Martin.

Scan the QR code below to join my email newsletter or visit JinceyLumpkin.com/Front-Matter

facebook.com/jinceylumpkin

twitter.com/jinceylumpkin

instagram.com/storiesbyjincey

To request permissions, contact the publisher at jincey@jinceylumpkin.com

Ebook: 978-1-7376155-3-8
Print: 978-1-958452-01-1
Hardcover: 978-1-958452-00-4

CIP Block/Library of Congress Number:
1-11719756291

First edition September 2022.

Edited by Amanda E. Clark
Cover art by Jason Brooks
Cover art direction by Matthew Axe
Cover layout by Lauren Balistreri

For my beloved friend, Sekiya.

Your grace, talent, and dedication to your craft are an inspiration to me.
May all of our dreams come true.

ACKNOWLEDGMENTS

Mermaid of Monte Carlo was, by far, the most challenging book to write. I now understand why some authors fail to complete their series. It's daunting work, to be sure. You have to push the characters and the plot to the breaking point, without actually breaking them.

There's definite sadness as I complete this, the sixth and final book in my Mermaid of Venice series. However, I am comforted by the fact that, while this is the natural ending point for Gia's story, there is still so much to explore in this universe that I've created. These characters have become my friends and companions, and I know I will return to them time after time.

I absolutely could not have finished this book without Amanda, my editor. Amanda, you wrapped a big proverbial rope around my waist and helped pull me through. I will always be grateful for your insights and ideas.

My deepest thanks to Matthew Axe, Jason Brooks, and Lauren Balistreri for my gorgeous book covers. I can't wait to have all six on my bookshelf together.

A big thank you to my beautiful wife, Eva, for coming in with her silly action movie ideas just when I need them. Plus, Eva, you balance me out and drag me away from the computer when I need to breathe fresh air.

And to my readers, I hope I've entertained and titillated you during this twisty journey with *Signorina* Gia Acquaviva. Stick with me... I've got a lot more rabbits in my top hat.

CONTENT ADVISORY

This book contains intense descriptions of graphic sex, violence, and abuse, including emotional abuse, murder, and torture.

MERMAID OF MONTE CARLO

1

July 13th

The supermoon occupied nearly all the sky over Stone Mountain, just east of Atlanta, Georgia. Set atop the lone granite monadnock was a wooden podium, and behind the podium stood former U.S. President, Ronnie Spade.

He loomed over the crowd, a menacing force.

"Hello, my good people!" he barked.

His supporters hooted back at him, elated.

"I asked the goons in our government about putting my face on Mount Rushmore, but they said, 'Oh, Ronnie, it can't be done. The park is too old... the carvings are falling apart.' But being here with all of you Georgia Peaches, I realize that maybe it's better to be memorialized where we stand! Who wants to see my face engraved onto Stone Mountain, alongside these fine Confederate leaders?"

He gestured to the large bas-relief below him, and the crowd howled, signaling their approval.

"These Confederate generals... they don't make 'em like that anymore, do they?" he crowed. "They came from a time when men were respected for being men!"

"WE LOVE YOU, RONNIE!" an old, white-haired Baby Boomer screamed, like she was watching The Beatles for the first time on The Ed Sullivan Show.

He yelled back at her. "Ronnie loves you, too, sugar!"

Laughter thundered through the crowd, and Ronnie soaked up all the adulation. Speaking at rallies was always his favorite part of campaigning. He didn't care too much for the actual governing that was part and parcel of being elected, though. If it were up to Ronnie, he would have done away with Congress and given buzzers to everyone at his rallies. That way, *his* people could vote for the policies *they* wanted.

He'd gone so far as to suggest that very governing approach to his Chief of Staff. Ronnie thought of the idea as a bold, new initiative... something to try once he'd won re-election. The Chief of Staff was baffled by the ex-president's suggestion and was forced to explain to Ronnie that passing legislation in America didn't work that way. The country is a representative democracy... or it's supposed to be, anyway.

Ronnie was highly annoyed. However, that night on Stone Mountain, he had bigger fish to fry.

The crowd was transfixed by his blonde wig, because the moonlight reflected off of it like a glow-in-the-dark tuft of cotton candy.

Ronnie yelled into his mic, "I don't like seafood, do you?"

"NO!" the crowd replied.

"Yeah, it smells. It's dirty! And... let's be honest... nothing tastes as good as a well-done American cheeseburger! Am I right?"

His supporters started chanting, "CHEESE-BUR-GER, CHEESE-BUR-GER," but Ronnie floated his hands in mid-air, quelling the noise.

"Do you know what's happening *right now* at the Pentagon?" Ronnie continued. "Our generals and our brave men and women in uniform are taking orders from *mermaids!* Mermaids in the Pentagon? African mermaids, no less! Can you imagine? They have this airy fairy, light-in-loafers African merman and his mama up there ordering our generals around. And for what? Magic! I don't know about you, but that seems like satanic stuff to me. *Magic...* ha! It's as if we are living in a liberal's wet dream of a Disney movie! Fish belong in the sea... or better yet... in an aquarium! But not in the government, *never* in the government! I won't stand for it!"

He paused for a moment to survey the audience. They were on his hook, eager for his next words, and ready to direct their collective rage anywhere he sent it.

Ronnie leaned forward, shouting into the mic, sending spittle flying. "We need to stop the people who are aiding the mermaids and take back our country. OTN and Harper Langley have been pushing this unnatural, un-American agenda. I want you all to join me next week in New York City. We're going to storm the OTN offices and teach little Harper Langley a lesson! It's gonna be wild!"

2

July 14th

Outside Athens, Greece, at a decommissioned American military base, a plane carrying high-ranking Pentagon personnel touched down. The first to exit the plane was the Chairman of the Joint Chiefs of Staff, General G. Henry Thomas.

Parked on the tarmac was a black sedan with tinted windows. General Thomas cracked open the car door to find Queen Mother Awa Diop and *La Nonna* waiting inside.

Awa offered a handshake as Thomas climbed in. "General, it is lovely to see you again. Let me introduce you to Gia Acquaviva's attorney, Donatella Sapiente."

"Please," the old woman interjected, "call me *La Nonna*. Everyone does."

The general nodded in her direction, tipping his service cap. "I'm General Thomas, and I am very much looking forward to working with you, *La Nonna*."

"*Bene, allora...* I am not sure that we *will* work together, General Thomas. You see, I have not received any formal offers for my client.

Forgive me if I reserve a healthy skepticism of the U.S. government. When it comes to criminal law, sir, I do not trust verbal agreements."

"That is understandable, ma'am. Let me assure you, our interest in Gia Acquaviva and her daughter is coming directly from President Bowden. He has given me explicit instructions to strike a beneficial deal with you. We would like to bring Ms. Acquaviva and her child over to the States as soon as possible. Project Blue Whale is a top priority for the president."

La Nonna scrunched her nose, confused. "Project Blue Whale?"

"Apologies, ma'am. This is what we call the initiative we're working on with Queen Mother Awa."

"I see. And what is the *nature* of this project?"

"That's classified, ma'am."

La Nonna chuckled. "Ah, but of course it is. You Americans do love your secret little files!"

The general stared at her blankly, which made her laugh even harder.

Awa cleared her throat, interrupting *La Nonna*'s giggles. "Let's not keep Gia waiting any longer. I suggest we get a move on. After all, the clock is ticking."

3

July 14th

East of Crete, in the deepest part of the Mediterranean, the riptide curled its icy fingers around Queen Zale. Here, in the sunken sea, everything was dark, except for the thousands of small, glowing eyes that encircled Zale the Ancient.

She had communed with the Gracious Tides in Cold Currents over these last many months. The shivering whispers had shared many secrets of old with the silver-haired queen. She was plump with knowledge and eager to do the bidding of her gods.

She had but one desire: to break open Serena and unleash the full force of the power that was contained inside the child.

A many-eyed beast, the Gracious Tides could view any place in the world through a single droplet of water. That meant there was no hiding for little Serena. The Gracious Tides knew exactly where the child was being kept, and they murmured to Queen Zale that the time had come to collect the girl.

"*La Plage Bleu,*" the voices chittered. "The men are hiding the child in a house near Marrakech."

Then they conjured shapes in the water: the coast, a beach, a white riad covered in sparkling tiles.

"Yes," Zale said, bearing a toothy grin, "I see her."

* * *

VITTORE SURVEYED the landscape outside of the window of the riad. The sky above the beach was overcast, and he frowned. He glanced down at Serena, who was playing on a carpet at his feet. "No beach for you today, my baby." Then he turned his head and yelled for Stavros, "*Dolce mio!* Come, please."

Stavros came pattering into the room from the kitchen. "What do you need, my young lover? I am preparing a basket of food to take to the beach."

"There are too many clouds. Our Father in the Sky must be unhappy today. There will be rain later."

"Rain?" Stavros grumbled. "In Morocco... in July? I think not."

Vittore moved away from the window and pushed Stavros toward it. "See for yourself, you old mule."

"How strange," Stravros said, peeking outside.

Vittore threw his hands up.

Stavros kissed his fiancé on the cheek. "How about a visit to the famous market instead?"

"I am not sure it is safe to be in the streets with Serena," Vittore replied. "What if someone recognizes her?"

"Recognizes a one-year-old baby? That is unlikely. Anyway, we can cover her up in the stroller. I cannot spend another day in the house, Vittore. I believe cabin fever has set in."

Vittore exhaled deeply and finally said, "Very well, then." He smiled as he spoke to Serena. "*Sirenetta*, shall we prepare the camels for the journey?"

Stavros hugged Vittore, because he was delighted by their plan. "I will tell the driver and the guards that we are leaving."

* * *

STAVROS PUSHED Serena's carriage through rows upon rows of colorful shops in the Marrakech souk. Vittore marveled at a collection of copper lamps dangling precariously over their heads.

"It was a good idea to get out, was it not?" Stavros asked, fishing for a compliment.

Vittore stretched his lips out, so he looked like a frog, and then he poked his tongue out a few times, as if to catch flies.

Stavros rolled his eyes and laughed to himself. The men stayed close together, guarded on either side by two of Shadow's hard men.

They reached an open section of the market and discovered a café. "Shall we sit for a coffee?" Stavros asked.

Vittore nodded, and they each took a seat at a small table. Vittore took hold of the baby carriage and scooted it closer to him. Serena was snuggled inside, napping. The sight of her sweet face tugged at a tender place inside his soul. "I love you with all my heart, *sirenetta mia*. And how I miss your mamma. I wish she was here with us now."

Stavros reached out and caressed his lover's cheek. "Soon. If I know anything about Gia, I know that she cannot be locked away for long. She is a very powerful and capable woman, Vittore. She will find a solution. I am sure of it."

Vittore swallowed a lump in his throat and nodded, putting on a brave face.

Suddenly, the wind picked up and blew their napkins off the table. Stavros jumped up and scurried after them. The wind blew harder, and several oranges were pushed off a nearby fruit stand. One of them rolled along the floor and landed at Vittore's feet.

A few fat droplets of water fell, hitting the men on the head. "Stavros, I told you it was going to rain!" Vittore shouted, rising from his seat. "Take cover!"

Commotion broke out as the shopkeepers packed away their goods, and customers rushed to find shelter. The rain came clattering down in thick, rumbling sheets.

A clap of thunder boomed so loudly that it shook the ground beneath their feet. Serena awoke, howling in fear. Vittore peeled back the cover and took her hand, trying to soothe her.

One guard spoke to the men. "Would you like to wait this out or return to the car?"

Stavros and Vittore exchanged a worried glance before answering.

"Maybe it is better to wait in the car," Vittore replied.

"As you wish, sir." The guards began clearing a path for the men, snaking through throngs of people. The rain was so fierce that it caused streams of water to flow through the market. Thunder and lightning continued thrashing and popping outside.

"What a storm!" Stavros shouted.

"Indeed!" Vittore replied, looking at his young charge with worry.

Serena was really screaming now, and Vittore very much wanted to pick her up and carry her, but he felt it was safer to leave her in the baby carriage where she was.

They all turned down a skinny alleyway, rushing to the car. Once they were out in the street, they saw how massive the storm really was, and it stopped them cold in their tracks.

The sky was deep purple, and the dark clouds seemed to knock against each other, sparking as they touched. The wind blew so intensely that it snapped a tree in half. In the distance, they saw a cyclone barreling down toward the market.

Vittore panicked and fled back into the alleyway with the stroller. Stavros and the guards followed. The wind howled its deep growl as it grew more intense by the minute. The guards swept the group into a merchant's stall, and they all crouched behind a counter.

But the storm found them anyway.

First, they heard ripping sounds as fabric awnings were tossed about as if they were flimsy paper towels. Then came the ping-ping-ping of objects as they rattled against the stucco walls. Finally, there were intense noises—the breaking of walls, the crushing of stones.

The squall had arrived.

The roof was torn off the section of the market where Vittore and Stavros were sheltered. The base of the cyclone twisted, wrapping everything into its hungry arms.

Finally, something heavy fell from the sky and hit Vittore's head, knocking him unconscious.

Serena screamed with newfound fear and fury.

4

July 14th

To say that the Greek police were unenthusiastic about experiencing American intervention in their detention of Gia would be an understatement. In fact, the Greek government and its criminal authorities outright resented General Thomas and his backing by the President of the United States. They found it offensive that the Americans believed it appropriate to waltz in and poach their catch of the century.

Therefore, the prison guards acted with intense hostility as they escorted the American-led entourage through the jail and into the private meeting room where they had Gia shackled by her hands and feet to a hard metal chair.

"Gentlemen," General Thomas began, "let's uncuff Miss Acquaviva."

The guards exchanged suspicious glances and muttered to each other in Greek.

Gia listened, offered a sarcastic snort, and translated as she rolled her eyes. "They are worried that if they let me loose, I will strike them down with magic. It is ridiculous."

General Thomas raised the volume of his voice and said, "Please uncuff her *now*. I will take full responsibility for her behavior."

One guard huffed and fumbled with keys on a ring, taking his sweet time in letting Gia loose.

La Nonna, Queen Awa, and General Thomas took their seats at the table with Gia. The general's underlings lined up against the wall.

"It is a pleasure to meet you, Miss Acquaviva. I hope the Greeks have been treating you with respect."

Gia eyed General Thomas with suspicion before answering him.

La Nonna spoke instead. "General Thomas has offered a verbal agreement to grant a transfer of custody to the United States."

Gia leaned back in her chair and crossed her arms over her chest. "In exchange for Serena, as I understand."

"Exactly this," *La Nonna* replied.

Gia turned her head and spoke in Italian to *La Nonna*. "What if I do not agree?"

La Nonna also gave her response in Italian, rushing through her points. "I think that would be unwise, *angioletta*. The Greeks have been... *uncooperative* in my attempts to extradite you to Italy. And more than that, they appear uninterested in the most basic application of their criminal code in your case. I believe they plan to give you harsh punishment and take advantage of the media exposure that your case is bringing them. *Signorina* Acquaviva, I hate to tell you, but public opinion about your kind has shifted radically since the destruction of Venice. The people of the world are standing at their shores with metaphorical fishing nets, ready to capture any mermaid who might pop up from the sea. Furthermore, the Greeks have a personal vendetta because you destroyed their little island in the Cyclades with your infighting."

Gia exhaled and spoke to the general. "Sir, if I may, what interest does the American government have with an infant?"

"Ma'am," Thomas replied, "your child is not an average baby. From what King Moussa described, she possesses the powers of necromancy and resurrection. Surely you can appreciate the interest that history's greatest military superpower has in such a magnificent thing as that. We feel that Serena could prove to be highly useful. A game changer, really."

Gia clenched her jaw as she felt her blood boil and her gills ripple under her prison jumpsuit. "I see. And what makes you think that a mother would use her own child as a bargaining chip, General Thomas?"

The general narrowed his eyes as a sardonic smile played at the corners of mouth. "We know that you are not the *average* mother, Miss Acquaviva. Let's put aside the scores of accusations against you for murder. As a businesswoman, we are certain that you recognize a good deal when you see one. Are we wrong?"

Gia let out one dry laugh. "What a pitch."

The general shrugged. "Look, Miss Acquaviva, let me put it to you in even more simple terms. We can do this the easy way or the hard way. It's up to you. The easy way is a win-win. The hard way is not. Regardless, we *will* get what we want. We always do."

"Pardon me?" Gia sneered. "Is the U.S. government in the business of kidnapping babies now?"

"Ma'am, we are in the *business* of protecting our interests at any cost."

Gia turned her gaze to *La Nonna* and stared at the old woman for quite a long time before responding. *La Nonna* offered no words of advice or comfort. She'd already said her piece.

This was a dead end road.

Gia closed her eyes and swallowed. "General Thomas, you have a deal."

5

July 15th

Queen Zale held Serena close to her bosom. They were suspended together in the eye of the storm, floating in a sort of protected bubble. Serena screamed and sobbed, but the wind masked her cries. Night and day they traveled through the sky like this, carried along by the power of the Gracious Tides.

When they finally dipped back into the deep sea and entered Cold Currents, Serena had gone eerily quiet. Zale was worried the child might die.

At the throne of the Gracious Tides, the eyes of the beast gathered around Serena, examining her.

* * *

Vittore awoke with a throbbing headache. He found himself in a hospital bed with Stavros by his side.

He lost his breath. "What has happened?"

"Shh," Stavros petted his head. "Please, try to rest."

"Rest!? Old man, you must tell me this instant where I am and what happened. Where is Serena?" he demanded, terror in his voice.

Stavros gritted his teeth. "My love, she is gone."

"Gone?! Gone where? What do you mean?!" Vittore began pawing at the cords attached to him, struggling to get up and out of bed.

"Stop that!" Stavros shouted. "That does no good."

Tears rushed out of Vittore's rheumy eyes. "Is Serena dead?"

Stavros hesitated. "I... I am not sure."

"Father in the Sky! Not sure?" Vittore prayed under his breath. So rushed was he in his recitations that he wheezed.

"Please lie down, Vittore," Stavros insisted. "I will explain everything."

Of course, Vittore did not lie down. Instead, he crossed his arms and tried to stop himself from crying by scowling at Stavros and focusing on his fury.

Stavros folded himself into a chair next to the bed. "What happened was strange. The storm came right to us. It knocked you out. Serena was sucked up by the cyclone. But as soon as that happened, the storm became dead silent. There was wind, of course, but no sound. The cyclone retreated, bouncing high into the sky, as if it disappeared into the clouds. It was as if the storm came specifically with the intent to take Serena."

Vittore stared off into the distance, pondering this new information, trying to imagine such a thing. His shock was so great that he could not speak.

There was a sinking feeling in his heart. Stavros understood what Vittore felt, because he felt it, too.

Inside, they both knew that the storm had indeed come for Serena. And they feared that whatever or whomever stole her planned to subject her to a fate worse than death.

6

July 15th

"...And then, apparently, she was taken into the storm. The authorities have been searching the area around the market, but they have not found Serena's body."

La Nonna paused, studying Gia's face to see if her client had absorbed the gravity of the bad news.

Gia stared at *La Nonna*, but remained silent. In fact, Gia wasn't even breathing. At some point during the last few moments, as *La Nonna* had explained that Vittore was in the hospital and Serena was missing, Gia had completely shut down. The only people she truly loved were in trouble—and in Serena's case, possibly dead—and Gia was trapped in a crumbling Greek jail. She felt helpless.

Gia hated feeling helpless.

"*Signorina* Acquaviva?" *La Nonna* reached across the table to try to comfort Gia. As the old woman's hand neared Gia's, she jerked away, reflexively pulling her hands into her lap.

After several moments of silence, Gia finally spoke.

"I want to see Shadow," she said.

La Nonna grimaced. "I am not sure that will be allowed."

An intense rage exploded inside Gia, and she balled up her fists to keep from screaming. She leaned over the table, bringing her body as close to her lawyer as the shackles around her would allow.

"Old woman," she hissed in a whisper, "I do not *care* how it is achieved, but I want you to coordinate with Shadow and get me out of this fucking place. *Immediately.*"

La Nonna nodded.

Gia sat back and closed her eyes, trying to catch her breath and calm herself. "I will not be of any use to the Americans without Serena. What you described to me about the storm in Morocco is no natural phenomenon. Tornadoes made of water do not kidnap children. Sea witches do. In Venice, I saw with my own eyes what Queen Karen is capable of doing. She took Serena. I know it! With Shadow's help, I will find my baby. Once I have her in my arms, I will then decide how best to protect her."

La Nonna sighed. "Then I will try to hold off the Americans until we know more about Serena."

Gia nodded.

The truth was that a cloud of doom shrouded both women. Neither was convinced that Serena would be all right.

* * *

QUEEN ZALE SWADDLED Serena in a seaweed wrap and let the merbaby float in the water. The Gracious Tides swayed Serena back and forth to relax her into sleep.

A thousand voices spoke at once, filling Zale's ears with their whispers. "Break open the child," the Gracious Tides commanded. "Release her power, and we will drink in the magic together. Zale the Ancient, claim your rightful throne among the Gods of Old."

Zale raised her arms, hovering them in the air amidst her flowing silver hair. She could feel energy surging through her body. She focused on the intense throbbing power and concentrated it in her fingers as she chanted malevolent incantations, words of destruction.

She placed her hands on Serena's head and squeezed.

A great golden wave emanated from the child. It was a current so forceful that it knocked Zale down, throwing her far away.

Serena awoke, shrieking. She was glowing with bright golden light.

The Gracious Tides howled and picked Zale up from the seafloor. "The child is marked by the sun."

"Marked by the sun," Zale echoed.

The many eyes of the Gracious Tides swirled around Zale. Their voices chanted, "The moon, the moon, the moon."

Inside her mind's eye, Zale saw the images that the Gracious Tides projected. The moon flashed in an instant, silver and cold. And then, rising out of the surface of the moon, was a great staff carved from moon quartz. Next, the Gracious Tides showed her the Salt Cathedral and whispered instructions in a long-forgotten language.

Zale smiled in satisfaction.

"O Gracious Tides, make of me your servant. Fill me with your power. I am a hungry child at your tender bosom."

There was no doubt about what Zale needed to do next. She had to convince Queen Karen to bring her that magical scepter made of moon quartz. Zale needed the Moon Staff to break the spell that protected the child.

7

July 16th

"I'm coming to you this evening with breaking news," Harper Langley said, staring at the camera lens. "Our sources have confirmed that top Pentagon officials are entering into an agreement with the world's most infamous mermaid, the alleged serial killer, Gia Acquaviva. The terms of the agreement are unclear, but what we do know is that the Greek government may soon relinquish Gia Acquaviva from its custody and hand her over to American authorities."

The camera pulled back to a wider shot, revealing two guests on either side of Harper. "Here with me in the studio are two people you have likely seen before." The camera transitioned to a different angle, and a striking woman in her thirties nodded hello. The on-screen graphics below the woman read, "Paula Fernández, the sister of Nicolás Ángel Fernández, who was allegedly Gia's most famous murder victim."

Harper gave a consoling glance to Paula and then said, "Paula Fernández, thank you for joining me once again here at OTN."

Paula wore an expression that conveyed her displeasure.

"I really hesitated about coming back on your show, Harper. My entire family feels betrayed by you. After the death of my brother, you used us... used our grief to drive up your ratings, and when it suited you, you turned on us and joined forces with Gia Acquaviva and the mermaids."

Harper smirked and shot back at Paula. "At OTN, we give people the simple truth. The facts, Paula. And at that time, the facts did not line up as you and I might have hoped they would. Back then, we didn't have the mountain of evidence that we now have, showing a high likelihood that Gia killed your bro—"

"Our Truth Network?" Harper's other guest, Iris Cutler, piped in, interrupting the host. "It's funny how much you lie here on OTN considering your network's supposed commitment to the *concept* of the truth."

With a smile, Harper replied, "So says the head of the re-election campaign for the most infamous liar ever to grace... or should I say *disgrace*... the White House, Ronnie Spade."

Iris faked a grin. "The president misses you, Harper. He is very hurt that you are no longer friends."

"The *ex-president* has no *real* friends." Harper tilted her head like an aggressive ostrich. "You know that, Iris. He only has ass-kissers." Then she turned her attention back to her main camera, addressing the viewers. "Wow, I didn't know that I was going to be attacked non-stop on live television, my friends. But never mind that. Let's refocus our discussion back to the major story for the evening... the explosive report that the Pentagon is dealing directly with Gia Acquaviva."

Harper waited a beat and then looked over at Iris. "What do you make of this news, Iris?"

Iris shrugged. "The bottom line is that mermaids are dangerous predators, Harper. Poor Paula knows that better than anyone. Gia Acquaviva *allegedly* slit Paula's gorgeous brother's throat like it was nothing. She cut him like she was gutting a fish. Everyone who comes into contact with that woman... that *creature*... faces a dance with death. America is about strength. *We're* supposed to be the sharks.

But the sad generals over at the Pentagon are nothing but a school of little guppies."

Paula spoke next. "I have been in contact with the families of Gia's other victims. It has been so difficult for them not to know what happened to their loved ones. The Mermaid File finally revealed the truth. We all want Gia to be punished for what she has done. If the plan is for the American government to bring her to justice, then we support those efforts."

Harper opened her mouth to speak, but was interrupted by Iris before she could get a word out.

"Harper, honey, we all know how much you *love* your mermaid buddies, especially that African one... but the American people... hell, the citizens of the entire world have had it with mermaids. Just ask the survivors of the flood in Venice."

"I will concede," Harper replied, "that public sentiment has been very anti-Mermaid as of late. We see it in our OTN social media comments and in our email inboxes. People are furious."

Iris lifted her finger. "And rightfully so! Mermaids are a serious threat to civilization as we know it. We don't even fully understand what they are capable of. Which is why, Harper, President Spade wants to know why you keep giving airtime to mermaid propaganda?"

Harper rolled her eyes. "Mermaid propaganda? Hardly. OTN believes that to get to the truth, you have to hear from both sides."

"Sure, sure," Iris chided. "Says Gia Acquaviva's mouthpiece."

Harper's face turned red. "I am no one's mouthpiece!"

Iris glared down the barrel of the camera. "People of America, Ronnie Spade has had it! On July 19th we invite you to a protest with us outside the OTN office here in Manhattan to call on Harper Langley and the rest of the media to stop promoting these anti-American Mermaids. It's time to take our power back. Fish belong in aquariums, not in government. Kill the fish!"

Harper stood up from the desk and shouted at her producer, "Cut the feed!"

8

July 16th

Queen Karen fiddled with the light switch in her quarters at the Japanese colony. She grunted before gritting her teeth and speaking to the AI bot that controlled the functions of the room. "Turn off the lights."

A chipper robot voice responded in Japanese as it made the lights even brighter.

"I said turn them off, damn it!"

The robot voice replied, but Karen couldn't understand it.

"Every night is the same fucking routine!" She slammed her hand down on the light switch several times, and the lights finally flickered off.

Lowering herself into her sleeping pod, Karen struggled to make her long body fit into the petite egg. Exasperated, she swung her legs out and huffed. She reached for her water glass, which was precariously balanced on a small shelf that slid out from the wall beside the sleeping pod.

As she brought the glass to her mouth, she noticed some kind of strange shape present on the surface of the water.

"What in the hell?"

She opened a drawer in the wall and fumbled for her reading glasses. Once they were on, and she could finally see what she was looking at, she gasped.

It was Queen Zale's face in the water.

Karen dropped the glass, and it shattered on the concrete floor. From the puddle that was left behind, Zale's form emerged.

Zale's water hologram spoke. "My sister queen, fear not."

Karen was never rattled by much, but the sight of a woman she assumed was dead caused her to shiver. Was she seeing a ghost, or had cabin fever set in after too many days in such cramped quarters?

"Are you real?" Karen asked Zale.

"The Gracious Tides bid you good eve, Queen Karen."

Karen blinked a few times. She considered the thought that perhaps she was having some kind of lucid fever dream.

Zale's hand reached out and stroked Karen's cheek. She could feel how cold and wet the woman's touch was, and she realized that what was happening was, in fact, real.

"Queen Karen, I seek your aid. Should you join my quest, an eternal reign shall be your reward."

"A reward? What are you talking about, Zale?"

"I have the child, Queen Karen. I am holding Serena in Cold Currents. The Gracious Tides are guiding me, and I have seen what must be done. I need you to bring me the Moon Staff. Together, at the Salt Cathedral, we will sacrifice the child."

Karen looked at Zale, feeling dumbfounded.

"I don't know what the Moon Staff is," Karen replied.

Zale's figure twisted, transforming into a tall, slender stick with a replica of the moon carved into the handle.

Zale's soft voice fluttered around the room. "The Archivist keeps the Moon Staff locked away in a collection of magical objects. Upon the next full moon, come to the Salt Cathedral and bring the staff. With it, we shall break the child's wards and harness the power she holds inside."

Before Karen could ask further questions, Zale's specter vanished, and water once again splashed onto the floor of the room.

Karen stared at the puddle, a smile toying at the edges of her mouth.

"Well, shit. What a development."

9

July 18th

Gia poked at a plate of cold food inside her cell. There was a slab of dry white meat next to oily potatoes. From the smell of it, the meat was some kind of practically rotten fish. She squeezed her eyes shut and nibbled on the corner of a potato slice. The potato had absorbed all the flavor of the fish, and she gagged. Without hesitation, she grabbed the plate and flung it to the floor.

She collapsed onto her bed and curled into a ball. Tired and starving, she longed to escape.

As she laid there feeling sorry for herself, Gia wondered how much longer she would be trapped in jail, when suddenly she smelled smoke. She bolted upright and jumped from her cot, rushing to the door of her cell, looking out the small window into the hallway. A plume of black smoke floated through the air.

There were screams in the distance. "*To spíti épiase fotiá!*" A cacophony of voices all yelled the same thing: "The jail is on fire!"

An alarm siren screeched to life, wailing and flashing its lights.

Gia could hear total chaos unfolding around her. More screams, rushing, the pounding of fast footfall.

Then an announcement over the loudspeaker: *"ÉNARXI TON DIADIKASIÓN EKKÉNOSIS!"*

Gia's heart was close to beating out of her chest, because she knew exactly what they were saying.

The prison guards were ordering everyone to evacuate.

Click.

The lock on Gia's cell door opened. She slid it to the side and poked her head out. The scene in the hallway was sheer madness. Guards tried their best to usher prisoners to safety. However, the smoke was thicker now, and it was becoming difficult to see.

Gia coughed, ducking under the smoke as well as she could to make her exit down the hallway. She joined a line of women headed toward the prison yard. As they turned the corner, they were met by a crowd of other prisoners, and the crush of bodies made it impossible to move.

The smoke was choking everyone, and Gia found it difficult to breathe. The air was filled with particles that clawed at and clogged her throat. She gasped for air and tried to shove her way through the crowd.

To the left, Gia heard the loud clanging of metal on metal. The sound rang in her ears and she strained to see what it was. She saw a thick metal door bending at its seams, and she wondered if the fire was making it collapse into itself.

But no—she heard voices coming from the other side of the door. The sharp end of a halligan pried its way through the door, opening a hole. Light pierced into the hallway.

Firefighters ripped the door from its hinges and pulled prisoners out one by one. Gia pushed herself close to the doorway. Her body craved breathable air.

But just as she reached the exit, some blunt force knocked her on the head and stars danced around her field of vision. Blood poured down her face, dripping into her eyes. She tried wiping it away, but that only made it worse. She couldn't see a thing, and as much as Gia wanted to scream, she found herself unable to.

Someone pushed her, and she fell to the ground. She felt an intense pain shoot through her leg as she was trampled and she felt her bone fracture. Between the blood, the smoke, and the pain, she could barely breathe.

And then she felt her body being lifted from the ground. It happened so fast. Gia was scooped up and thrown over a man's wide shoulder. He ran with her for quite some time. The screams and alarms were muted by the sound of rushing water from the firemen's hoses.

The man holding her slowed down a bit and turned around a few times. He must have been confused about which way to go. Gia wasn't sure. The blood stung her eyes, so she kept her eyelids closed—she willed herself to stay conscious and not pass out from the pain.

"This way, boss!" someone screamed.

The man took a hard left. Gia heard little metal pops, too soft to be gunshots. Then she listened to the sound of squeaking metal and realized that the fence in the jailyard was being rolled up.

"Hang on a bit longer, Gia," the man holding her whispered.

She knew that voice.

It was Shadow.

Shadow's feet crunched on gravel, and then Gia's body flopped as he descended a long set of stairs. In the distance, she heard lapping water.

"You gotta swim, love."

Shadow jumped into the water with Gia still on his shoulder. He pulled her through the water, his tail flapping furiously.

As her own tail emerged, she felt the scales tickle across the broken bone in her shin, and she screamed in agony. In turn, she swallowed a large amount of sea water, and she gagged. Finally, she blinked and rubbed her eyes until she rinsed away the blood.

She tried kicking her tail, but the pain was so intense that she stalled.

Shadow took her in his arms and wrapped her under him, hugging her close.

With one arm and his strong tail, he propelled them far from the shore to a boat that was waiting in the distance. And despite the pain, Gia allowed herself a moment of respite and relief.

She was free.

10

July 19th

Harper sat in the makeup chair in her dressing room at OTN's Manhattan headquarters. Her glam team fussed about, readying her for the camera.

There was a knock at the door.

"Come in!" Harper yelled.

Harper's producer craned his head in. He grimaced as he delivered a message that he knew would not be well received. "I just got off the phone with our team over in Greece."

"Okay..."

He swallowed. "There was a fire at Gia's jail. And... uh... they can't find her."

Harper swatted the glam team away and whipped her body around to face the producer. "Can't find her as in... she's dead and they can't identify the body?"

He shook his head. "It appears as though she was able to escape."

Harper cursed to herself. "That fucking bitch. She always sneaks away!" Then she looked at the producer, narrowing her eyes. "Let's go on air in three minutes."

He nodded and scurried off.

"Out, please," Harper said, dismissing the glam team. When she was alone, she picked up her cell phone and dialed *La Nonna*.

The call went to voicemail.

"*La Nonna*, this is Harper Langley. Where the *fuck* is Gia?"

* * *

THE POLICE HAD SET up barricades on the steps of the OTN building. Many of Ronnie Spade's supporters were already camped out in the courtyard of the Midtown office and had been tailgating for hours. As more and more people trickled in, the crowd became rowdier, more aggressive, and angry.

They chanted, "Kill the fish!"

The signs they held read, "Fish Belong in Aquariums, Not Government!" and "Gut Harper Langley!"

A motorcade sped up Sixth Avenue and began honking as it reached the OTN office. The crowd erupted in applause.

Ronnie Spade retracted the roof of his Escalade and stood on the center console, somehow testing physics and raising his considerable body through the open hole. One of his lackeys handed him a fire-engine red loudspeaker.

"Hello, my beautiful people!" he yelled. "I knew you'd turn out for me today, and I love ya for it!"

Over the next few minutes, hundreds of supporters became thousands. He took out a t-shirt gun and catapulted red hats and shirts to the crowd. The people fought each other for the cheap merchandise like starry-eyed twenty-something single ladies snatching for a bride's bouquet.

Secret Service agents cleared a path through the crowd for Ronnie Spade to climb onto a small platform with a microphone and a *faux* presidential podium.

Ronnie leaned over the microphone and spoke.

"Well, thank you very much. This is incredible. Of course, OTN won't show the magnitude of this crowd. We have thousands and thousands of people here, and I just want them to be recognized. Turn the cameras please! These good people came from all over our country... all over the world, actually... to have their voices heard."

On his order, the camera operators did as they were told, taking in the sea of bodies. These were true fans with unbridled—and potentially unstable—passion for their leader.

Ronnie continued on. "We are angry! We are angry and disturbed about the direction of this great country, and we won't stand for it anymore, isn't that right?"

The crowd howled back at him, expressing their collective rage.

Ronnie raised his voice. "We're here today because we need to take back our country! These queerbo African mermaids don't belong in the Pentagon. OTN and Harper Langley have been nothing but a propaganda factory, pumping out un-American LIES! *Little Harper Langley* has an agenda, you know! Our generals have become weak. They have been corrupted by Harper and her thug fish friends. But we won't put up with that, will we? Oh, no! Harper's gonna learn a lesson. We have to fight! We have to fight like hell to save our country! So here's what we're gonna do. We're gonna walk up those stairs into the OTN office and we're gonna tell Harper Langley to stop fraternizing with fish OR ELSE! I'm counting on you to help me deliver this message. We need to be strong. We need to save our country, and we need to do it right now. Thank you!"

The guards whisked Ronnie away.

Emboldened, one supporter hopped the barricade, but the police detained him. Then another one jumped, and another. Pretty soon, the force of the crowd pushed against the barricade so hard that it knocked over a line of police. Reinforcements came in and tried to form a new defensive line to fight off the crowd, but it was all in vain. The police were outnumbered. One man dressed in military garb began firing rounds out of an AR-15. He was promptly gunned down, but not before injuring at least ten police officers. A steady stream of rioters broke through the barrier of law enforcement and busted through the front doors of OTN.

* * *

"So far, the Greek authorities have been unable to locate Gia Acquaviva," Harper said, speaking to the camera, seemingly unaware of what was happening just outside the studio doors.

Suddenly, commotion broke out behind the camera, and for the first time, Harper was interrupted in her broadcast. The producer ran to Harper as she sat at the desk, trying to discern what was happening.

"Harper," he tried to speak calmly, but his voice was speedy and shrill, "we have to take you to the secure room. Ronnie Spade sicced his fans on you, and they're on their way up the stairs right now!"

Guards encircled Harper and hustled her to the private hallways that led to OTN's panic room—which had been the brainchild of Bronwyn, who had always known that this day would eventually and inevitably come to pass.

But it was too late.

A string of heavily armed militia men broke open a locked door, ambushing Harper and the guards. They sprayed bullets, taking out Harper's security.

Harper's heart pounded, and she darted her eyes in every direction, seeking a way to escape. She was cornered, like a hunted animal... and she was certain she was going to die.

The last thing she saw was a bag being lowered over her head. Someone stuck her with a needle, and everything went black.

11

July 21st

Yet again, Queen Karen had been waiting days to see Togashi. Every day Akiko gave Karen the same spiel about Togashi being so engaged in research that it was impossible for Togashi to meet with her.

Quite frankly, Karen was fed up. She marched down to the Archives and planted herself like a statue, tapping her foot, at the front desk of the Great Library.

Akiko bowed her head, just as she did every morning. "*Ohayō*, good morning, Queen Karen."

"You can stop with all that deferential crap," Karen snapped. "You've been downright disrespectful. This is no way to treat a queen... keeping her waiting days on end because some dusty intellectual has been sniffing books."

Akiko forced a smile. "We are in luck. Togashi is available to meet with you today."

"Today, at what time?" Karen demanded.

"In fact, Togashi is already on the way here. If you don't mind, please wait a few more minutes."

Karen huffed and tapped her nails on the counter of the front desk.

Within half an hour, Togashi arrived and waved Queen Karen into the library's golf cart, which was overstuffed with books and scrolls. Togashi rearranged a few things to make space for Karen and then whizzed away with her, curling through the Great Library's spiral bookcases at top speed.

"It is a most auspicious day!" Togashi shouted. "I have made a startling discovery. A *true* breakthrough in my research."

"How interesting," Karen replied, feigning interest. "I wonder... would you show me your famed collection of magical objects?"

Togashi slammed on the brakes. Queen Karen lurched forward and had to extend her hands to keep from hitting the golf cart's plexiglass windshield.

"My *famed collection of magical objects?*" Togashi repeated Karen's words with great suspicion. "Famous according to *whom?*"

Karen shrugged. "You are the Archivist, are you not? The keeper of all things magical? In our circles that makes you pretty famous, honey. I just thought it would be nice to get a tour of your magical knick-knacks... that's all."

"Knick-knacks?" Togashi whispered, while making a sour face. "I would not know where to begin, Queen Karen. I have vast stores of magical objects."

"How about we start with the Moon Staff?"

Togashi shot Karen an incredulous look and growled, "How do you know about the Moon Staff?"

"Is it supposed to be a secret or something?" Karen asked, hoping her tone sounded innocent.

"I have *never* spoken of its existence! Not in three hundred years. *Not ever!*"

"All the more reason to show me, then. Wouldn't you say? You must be so eager to share your knowledge after keeping this secret for so long."

Togashi stayed silent for what felt like a long time. Queen Karen matched that silence, betting on the fact that the awkwardness might make Togashi feel compelled to speak.

She was right.

"The Moon Staff is sacred," said Togashi, finally. "I have kept it under my protection all this time."

Karen nodded her head in agreement, deciding to be straightforward. "I get that. I do. But here's the thing, Togashi... it's gotta come out of storage. I need it."

Confusion washed over Togashi's face. "Queen Karen, I do not understand."

There was no way around it, Karen had to tell Togashi the whole truth.

"Zale came to me in a vision. She told me that the Gracious Tides have been helping her. She has Serena Acquaviva, and she's got to use the Moon Staff to break some kind of spell and take control of Serena's power."

Togashi gasped. "Then it has begun."

"What's begun?"

"The war."

Karen scoffed. "Darlin', the war's been happening for a while now. You yourself sent troops to help me attack Gia in Venice."

"I am not speaking of a quarrel between mermaid factions. The gods are at war now."

"I really don't know what you're talking about, Togashi."

"I uncovered an ancient text weeks ago. I was finally able to finish translating it last night. It was a tale of three siblings, the Goddess of the Moon, the Goddess of the Sun, and the God of the Sea."

Karen stared at Togashi, trying to follow the story. "Mmm hmm... and?"

"The God of the Sea betrayed his sister and trapped her soul in the Moon Staff. As a punishment, the Goddess of the Sun banished her brother to the coldest, deepest part of the ocean... to Cold Currents. She then broke his spirit into a million pieces. You see, all this time we have thought that the Sky God is one deity, but in reality, there are two sisters, Sun and Moon, with intertwined powers. The

Gracious Tides is nothing but the evil fragments of their tempestuous little brother."

"Right," Karen nodded, trying—and failing—to sound interested in this new information. "Um... so, does that mean I get to see the Moon Staff... or not?"

12

July 22nd

It was a day of bittersweet reunions for Gia. Yes, she was technically "free," but she was also hiding aboard a borrowed mid-sized yacht, floating in the Aegean Sea—so it wasn't as if she had been returned to the life she longed for.

The first visitors to board the ship were Vittore and Stavros, whom she welcomed with tenderness. With her leg broken, Gia could not manage getting out of the stateroom, so Vittore climbed in bed alongside her. Stavros stood at the foot of the bed, while Shadow lurked near the door.

"*Tesoro mio, tesoro mio,*" Vittore sobbed, "please forgive me." He hugged her and buried his head into her shoulder.

"The poor man has been like this for days," Stavros explained. "He is heartbroken over losing Serena."

Gia wrapped her arms around him, love flooding through her veins. She stroked Vittore's hair and kissed him on the forehead. "Stop this, *Methusalamme.* You did nothing wrong."

Not too long after Vittore and Stavros arrived, three more guests sailed up to the ship: Queen Mother Awa, King Moussa, and Prince Kyle. Everyone crowded into Gia's room.

After exchanging hellos and concern over Gia's condition, Kyle spoke.

"My mother called me last night. She needs our help."

Gia's mood immediately soured at his words. Through gritted teeth, Gia said, "Your mother *needs our help?*" Then she cursed over and over in Italian until Vittore shushed her.

"Listen to what the boy has to say, Gia!"

Kyle lowered his head but spoke firmly, "Queen Zale is holding Serena in Cold Currents—"

"I knew it!" Gia screamed. "I knew that a sea witch was behind that storm! How can I *trust* your mother, Kyle? Ah? How do we know it is not her who took Serena? It is *exactly* the sort of thing she would do. In fact, she already tried to take her!"

Kyle raised his hands. "I know, I know. Trust me. Since Mother attacked the colony in Senegal, I haven't been able to support her. And I won't support her, okay? That's why I have been working with King Moussa to help you, Gia. My mother has an evil side. I've seen it first hand. But I know for certain she doesn't have Serena, because Mother is in Japan with the Archivist."

"Shadow," Gia called out, "please, can you ask the steward to bring me a bourbon on the rocks? I need a drink."

Shadow cocked his head. "Ain't good to drink when you're taking those pain pills, Gia."

"I completely agree!" Vittore said, giving Shadow a thumbs up.

"I am a grown woman, for the love of God. I can decide when to have a cocktail."

Shadow raised his eyebrow. "*One* cocktail."

Gia's nostrils flared. "I would make it myself, but I am confined to the bed, you see."

Shadow smiled at her and returned a moment later, drink in hand.

Moussa shuffled over to Gia and then asked, "How did you

manage to get a yacht? I thought the government froze your assets." He offered a small shrug to denote the space around them.

Gia gulped from the cup. "It is a mafia ship, King Moussa. It belongs to one of *La Nonna's* clients."

Moussa prickled at the mention of the mafia. "*Oh la la,*" he said sarcastically. "Let's hope that no one's husband has to die in exchange for the mafia helping you."

Gia winced. Among all the things that had happened in the past few years, Oumar's death was one of the events that she regretted very much—it was something that she wished she could make right, but knew that she could not.

"It's a shitty little yacht anyway," Moussa remarked, taking a step back, regarding the room with disdain. Kyle reached out for Moussa's hand and kissed it.

"Uncle?" Gia asked, deciding to change the conversation. "Would you take me to Cold Currents? I know you have been there." She swirled the ice in her glass around with her finger, feigning nonchalance.

Stavros shivered.

"Wait," Kyle said, "that's *not* the plan. Mother is supposed to meet Queen Zale at the Salt Cathedral during the next full moon."

Gia looked puzzled. "But the colony was destroyed, Kyle."

"I'm just telling you what she told me. Mother's supposed to go there with some artifact from the Japanese. Zale wants Mother to help her to... uh..." he paused before saying the next words, "um... to help her *sacrifice* Serena."

Gia dropped the glass of whiskey, spilling the remaining liquor all over her belly.

"No, no, no," Gia cried.

"Shhh," Vittore cooed. "We will not allow any more harm to come to that baby."

But Gia ignored him and tore into Kyle. "I still do not understand. Why the hell would your mother want *my* help? She has been trying to kidnap Serena for such a long time. This feels like another one of her traps."

"It's not, Gia. Apparently, the Japanese are worried that this is going to set off some kind of war between the gods."

"What?" she snapped.

Kyle shrugged. "I know... it sounds ridiculous."

Awa spoke for the first time. "It doesn't sound ridiculous to me. This power comes from somewhere, and Moussa is here with us *today* because of Serena's magic."

"There's one other thing," Kyle said, his mouth twisted into an awkward frown. "The Japanese think Serena is the Sun Goddess or Sky God reincarnated... something like that."

Vittore scrunched up his face. "Our Father is the Sky... is... *a mother?*"

13

July 26th

In the middle of the night, two ships met in the sea. A plank was extended from one to the other. As agreed, Queen Karen and Togashi carefully stepped across into Gia's boat.

Shadow had lifted Gia out of her bed and set her up on deck. She sat at a table, surrounded by her allies.

Prince Kyle rose to greet Queen Karen. "Hello, Mother." They exchanged a weak hug.

Karen nodded in Gia's direction. "Hey, there."

Gia scowled. "This is what you have to say to me? How *dare* you."

Karen rolled her eyes. "How dare *I*? How dare *you*! Are you aware that you are speaking to a *queen*?"

Queen Awa stepped in. "Ladies, I am aware that you have never been formally introduced. Please, let's reset. We all have to work together, you know."

"Aren't you the little diplomat?" Karen sniped.

The comment enraged Awa. "Do you want our help or not, you unscrupulous old wench?! I have had my fill of you! Queen to queen, I am here as a show of goodwill, hoping that by working together, we might ease tensions among our kind. But I will *never* forget who you are or forgive what you have done. So I suggest that you pack away your snide remarks and correct your uppity attitude. Is that understood?"

Karen crossed her arms across her chest and placed an expression on her face that showed that she'd "like to talk with a manager."

"Hmm," Karen replied, "from where I stand, you need my help more than I need yours. I don't really give a shit what happens to Gia's quarter-breed baby."

Vittore opened his mouth to shout at Karen, but Stavros pinched his thigh to stop him.

Gia glared at Karen, and Karen glared right back.

"The child," Togashi interjected, "must be protected at all costs."

"And what exactly is the plan in that regard, Togashi?" Queen Awa asked.

Togashi backed away. "I am merely a scholar. Queen Karen is the warrior, not I."

"I see," Awa replied. "Well, I am all ears, Karen."

Karen smiled and took her sweet time before speaking. "I've considered every aspect of this plan, and what I think is this. Togashi, you will give me the Moon Staff, I will meet Zale in the Salt Cathedral, and then before she has time to hurt the kiddo, you all bust in and take out Zale. Simple."

"Oh, yes," Awa replied, "it's very simple to... as you said... *take out* the most powerful sorceress of our time."

Queen Karen stared blankly at Awa. "I'll help you, obviously. Anyway, it's not like you can do magic."

Awa's eye twitched in anger.

Gia leaned forward. "Queen Karen, why should I trust you after what you did in Venice?"

"Honey, you don't have a choice. I'm the best hope you've got of getting your baby back."

* * *

IN THE BLACKNESS of Cold Currents, Zale watched as the Gracious Tides projected the conversation between Karen, Gia, and the allies. She learned of Karen's betrayal in real time.

But Zale wasn't concerned.

She knew exactly what to do.

Her many-voiced god whispered specific instructions into her ears.

14

July 27th

Shortly before nightfall, Gia, Shadow, and the others sailed into *Nisí Margaritarión,* Pearl Island, the former home of the Greek mermaid colony.

The moon was rising in the east, casting a shadowy glow across the ridged mountains. Gia sensed an odd energy hanging in the air. It seemed as though the island was coming alive, like a menacing creature was awakening from a long hibernation, ready to fight. Shadow felt the strangeness, too. Somewhere in the distance, there was a groaning sound, a low growl that shook the earth below their feet.

Shadow picked up Gia and helped her hobble toward the bay.

"Where is Karen?" Stavros asked as he climbed off the boat.

Awa, Moussa, and Kyle stepped onto the pearly sand of the beach, joining the others.

"Mother will be here," Kyle insisted. "Let's just give her a little more time."

* * *

SERENA HOWLED in Queen Zale's arms as Zale floated down the spiral staircase on the way to the Salt Cathedral. Having never birthed children, Zale found Serena's cries overwhelmingly loud and unnerving. She could not wait to be rid of the child.

"Shhh, shhh," Zale whispered, trying unsuccessfully to soothe the baby. "Soon you will be at peace."

Zale knocked three times before creaking open the large wooden doors of the Cathedral. She headed directly to the chancel and laid Serena on an altar intricately carved from a block of solid pink salt. Serena thrashed about, seeming to understand that she was in grave danger. Worried that the child would roll and fall off the altar, Zale tied the baby down with a length of rope and waited for Queen Karen to arrive.

* * *

SHADOW PACED AROUND THE BEACH, investigating everything to survey any possible threats. "We should go down there... before it's too late."

Gia's heart raced, and her throat felt dry. "We need Karen. We cannot fight Zale on our own."

Picking up on Gia's angst, Moussa eyed his lover and snapped. "Kyle, your *maman* better show up."

Kyle chewed his fingernails but did not reply to Moussa's snide comment.

Water splashed behind them in the crescent bay, and Karen's head popped from the surface. The Moon Staff was strapped to her back.

"What are you waiting for?" she shouted. "Get going. I'll see you in the Salt Cathedral."

And then Karen was gone.

Stavros led the way as they all dove into the deep waters below *Nisí Margaritarión*. Of course, the colony was in ruins. Many of its passageways were barred with fallen rocks, a dark reminder of the battle between the Ice Folk and the two evil queens.

Instead of making the turn to arrive at the colony's now-destroyed main avenue, Stavros led everyone in the opposite direction. The plan was to sneak into the colony from a side entrance and ambush Zale in the Salt Cathedral.

Gia's bones ached from her fracture, but she pushed herself through the pain. She had to swim much more slowly than she wanted to.

The deeper they all descended, the stranger the terrain became. The walls of the caves were covered in sharp, glowing barnacles and juicy, pulsating tentacles. They arrived at a narrow opening, a slit so thin that Gia was certain they could not fit through.

She stretched out her arms and tried to make her body as flat as possible. Her tail wobbled, propelling her slowly through the opening. The jagged critters lining the walls cut into her skin, scraping it off. She tried to force herself through anyway, but her struggle was futile.

Shadow grabbed her tail and yanked her back into the water next to him. Hot pain surged through Gia's body as her tail twisted, and she screamed.

But it wasn't only the pain that caused her to howl—it was also the fear of what might happen to her baby.

She knew that they were running out of time.

* * *

KAREN ARRIVED at the Cathedral's doors and knocked three times.

Zale opened the doors to let Karen in.

"You are late," Zale whispered. "I was concerned that you would not come." Her voice sounded eerie and sinister, and it caused a chill to creep up Karen's spine.

"Better late than never," Karen replied, stepping inside the entry.

Immediately, Zale bolted the doors to the Cathedral closed and began chanting.

Her whispers echoed around the room. At first her voice was as soft and dark as the fluttering of many moth wings. But Zale's tenor became more shrill as she sank deeper into a trance. She spun around the room, slowly at first, and then with great speed. Her chants sounded like a hurricane whistling through the curved edges of a conch shell.

Zale chittered in Atargatis and also in an ancient tongue older than time itself. The mysterious words she spoke were from the Language of Creation. The spell she sought to cast was the Song of Destruction.

She felt a bobbing current enter her body. Zale had invited the Gracious Tides to find a home inside of her, and they lifted her up.

The spell was working.

Karen watched from the ground as Zale floated to the top of the Cathedral and hung there, as if sleeping on the ceiling.

* * *

STAVROS CUT a straight line up through the water, racing back to the main entrance of the colony. Shadow swam closely behind.

Awa and Moussa took hold of Gia on either side and helped her glide through the water. They passed by large rocks and through small crevices until they reached the colony's main avenue. The street was now completely flooded, which was helpful, actually, because it was easier for Gia to swim than to walk.

When they finally arrived at the spiral staircase, they were once again on dry land, deep underground. Shadow threw Gia over his shoulder like he had at the jail, and they hustled down the stairs to the Salt Cathedral.

The time had come to face Zale.

* * *

TOGASHI WAS RIGHT ABOUT SERENA, Karen thought.

She could feel the magical essence radiating off of the child. Simply being in Serena's presence during the full moon made Karen feel stronger. Magic pulsed inside Karen's veins, and she felt drunk with power.

A thousand voices whispered behind her. Karen spun around but saw nothing.

When she turned back toward Serena, she came face to face with Zale.

Only it wasn't Zale anymore, not really.

The silver-haired queen's eye sockets had been stretched wide. They covered the length of her face on either side of her nose. Inside were thousands of pairs of tiny eyes, like a revolting insect.

Karen stumbled backward, suddenly terrified.

Zale hovered over Karen, her arms reaching out to unnatural lengths. Zale's tail split apart like a Hydra, becoming a thousand tales.

"Give it to me," the Zale-beast commanded. Her voice was deep and multi-toned, like every key of an organ being played at once. "Give me the Moon Staff."

15

July 27th

Stavros was the first to make it to the doors of the Salt Cathedral. He tried to push them open, but it was impossible. Zale had bolted them shut.

"Help me!" he screamed. Shadow placed Gia on the ground and ran to Stavros. Moussa, Awa, and Kyle joined the two men, all working together to force the doors open.

"Uncle Stavros, is there another way in?" Gia asked, voice trembling with fear and desperation.

"No."

"And you?" Awa asked, glancing over at Kyle. "Can you cast spells like your mother?"

Kyle grimaced. "I could try."

"I am going to take that as a no," Awa replied, turning back to Stavros. "Could we burn the doors open or use something to explode them?"

Gia stood upright as best as she could and pushed her way through the group. She began banging on the doors with both hands, yelling, "Open these doors right now! Give me my daughter!"

On the other side, Serena heard her mother's cries and wailed.

Inside the Salt Cathedral, Karen tore her eyes away from Zale's monstrous face and looked at the doors, wishing very much that they would open, so that she could escape, or at least not have to be alone with this new version of Zale.

"Sister Queen," Zale hissed, "give me the Moon Staff. Let us break open the child and drink of her powers. For in doing so, we shall become one with the Gracious Tides and rule for eternity."

However, the power that Zale was offering was not the sort of power Karen desired. She didn't trust the Gracious Tides. Furthermore, Karen liked her body just fine as it was, and had no interest in being mutilated by an evil multi-God.

The two queens were interrupted by more screaming from Gia, as well as heavy thuds coming from the other side of the doors. Stavros and Shadow had retrieved a large stalagmite from a collapsed passage nearby and were using it as a battering ram.

Zale flew to the door and placed her hands on it. As she chanted, a multitude of shrieks escaped her lungs.

Suddenly, the wooden doors became transparent. Gia and the others could see into the Salt Cathedral, but they were trapped outside.

They gasped when they saw Zale's disfigured body and her huge insect eyes.

While Zale was preoccupied, Karen set about casting a spell of her own. But Karen did not need to rely on the Gracious Tides for her magic tonight.

The spell she planned to cast was no ordinary water incantation; it was an ancient enchantment to awaken the magic of the Moon Goddess. A gift of protection from Togashi.

Karen uttered the words to herself. She waved her hands in a complex pattern, following the instructions she had read on Togashi's old scroll. Her hands glowed with silver light.

Zale swooped back toward the altar, determined to finish what she had started and sacrifice the child. But as she approached Karen, a beam of silver light struck Zale, making a hole in her tail. She yelped in pain and collapsed onto the floor.

Karen untied the rope around Serena. With one hand, she grabbed the Moon Staff, and with the other, she took Serena. She shot down the aisle of the Cathedral and unbolted the door.

The group beyond the doors rushed inside. Gia sprang forward and took Serena into her arms, hugging her tightly.

But before they could further immobilize Zale, the queen rose again, her extremities extending out to spread widely across the room. She hovered over them like a dark, serpentine cloud.

Zale opened her mouth, and a cascade of sea water poured out. The water swirled around them, holding them in place.

Each tried to swim away, but the grip of the Gracious Tides was too strong. Gia winced in pain and struggled against the current. Serena cried and cried.

Zale dipped down and plucked the Moon Staff from Queen Karen's hands.

"You are a traitor, Queen Karen, and you shall pay for your betrayal with your life."

Before Karen had a chance to scream, the Gracious Tides twisted her body like a rag, breaking her neck. She was instantly paralyzed. Water crawled into her mouth, snaked down her throat, and knocked around inside of her guts, expanding outward and crushing her organs. The icy fingers of the Gracious Tides squeezed around Karen's heart, choking it and stopping it from beating. Her lifeless body fell to the floor.

Kyle called out for his mother, but she was gone.

With the traitor to her cause out of the way, Zale turned her attention to the task at hand. She ripped Serena away from Gia. No matter how much Gia thrashed, she could not break free of the hold the Gracious Tides had on her.

"Please," Gia begged, "Queen Zale, do not do this. Serena is only a baby... a harmless little girl. Please, please, let her live. Take me instead."

Zale ignored Gia's pleas and sped to the altar with Serena. She put Serena down and wrapped both hands around the Moon Staff.

The staff glowed brightly, its powers activated by Karen's spell.

Zale chanted all the words that the Gracious Tides had commanded her to say. She lifted the staff, raising it over her head. With all her force, she brought the heavy staff down onto Serena's head, crushing it.

As Serena's head broke, so did the staff. A spray of silver light was released around the room.

Zale smiled. It was done. The sacrifice had been made.

Or so she thought.

The broken pieces of the staff reassembled themselves into the shape of a knife. That magic dagger hovered in the air for a moment, considering its target, before shooting toward Zale.

It thrust itself straight into her heart.

She wailed, and the sound of a thousand moans seeped out of her.

The knife turned around and around inside her chest like a corkscrew until it pierced her completely and popped out on the other side.

Queen Zale collapsed in a heap. The waters holding Gia and the others subsided.

Gia rushed to the altar, a scream trapped in her throat.

There, she found Serena's tiny head, crushed... shattered.

Gia couldn't look away from the blood. And she couldn't bring herself to touch Serena. Her thoughts cycled through all of her own kills. All the blood she herself had spilled. Her sorrow clawed inside of her, trying to escape.

But she couldn't cry. She couldn't scream.

Everyone was around her now. They were all crying. They touched her, tried to embrace her, but Gia was somewhere else. She felt as if she had floated off—as if her mind no longer was at home in her body.

And her body collapsed.

Then, it was as if time stopped, and Gia did not know how long she had laid in the arms of her allies.

She heard the voice of her mother.

I am here, Gia. I am here.

Gia wanted to die.

In fact, she tried to close her eyes and will herself to die, but it didn't work.

When she finally opened her eyes again, she was met with the strangest sight: her mother's face.

"Mamma?" Gia whispered. "Am I dead?"

"It's me, Mommy," the face said. "It's me, Serena."

16

July 27th

Harper listened to the squeaky wheel of her metal cell as it was twisted open.

It's lunchtime, she thought. *What will it be today? More hot dogs?*

Her captor popped open the hatch of his rural doomsday bunker and let the sun shine down on Harper.

She covered her eyes to let them adjust to the light.

Maybe this time he will have come down here alone.

Her heart raced at the thought.

No such luck. As always, her kidnapper was guarded by a friend who stood just outside of the bunker, holding an assault rifle.

Her captor climbed down a ladder and passed her a warm bowl of pork and beans.

"Now, what do you say, Little Harper Langley?" he needled.

"Thank you, sir," Harper replied, bowing her head as he had instructed her to do when he first brought her to this godforsaken place. "May God and America bless you."

"I love the sound of that!" he replied. "Almost makes a snowflake liberal like you fuckable." He leered at her, and Harper fought to resist the urge to gag. She really hoped she would never be considered to be "fuckable" by this hillbilly or any of his three-toothed friends.

"Almost!" he added, which made Harper's blood boil even more.

Regardless, Harper didn't have the energy to throw any snark his way. Furthermore, being on the receiving end of an AR-15 tends to bring about a sense of humbleness to anyone.

The man sat down on a stool across from Harper to watch her eat. "Tastes good, huh?"

She nodded. Obviously this was not one of the Michelin-starred restaurant dishes she was used to indulging in, but at least her captor fed her three square meals a day. Harper was well aware that things could be much worse for her. Besides, the routine of mealtime helped her keep track of how many days she'd been trapped.

Eight so far.

She couldn't help but wonder how many days would pass until she was free again. And she didn't want to think about the alternative —namely, that she would never get out.

17

"Serena?" Gia stared into the face that she had only ever known as her mother's.

I must be hallucinating, Gia thought.

But then the beautiful woman, the grown woman who looked to be around the age of twenty, laid down beside Gia in the Salt Cathedral.

"Hold me, Mommy," Serena begged. "I'm scared."

Her voice was sweet and soft, with an American accent. She sounded quite a lot like Harper, in fact.

Gia looked up at Uncle Stavros and Queen Mother Awa. "What has happened? I do not understand." She hoped that, as the elder merfolk in the room, they could provide insight into the strange magic they were all witnessing.

But they simply gawped at the situation unfolding in front of them.

"I have been alive for more than two centuries," Awa replied in a whisper, "and I have never seen *anything* like this."

Stavros shook uncontrollably, and his face appeared grey enough to blend in with his beard. He didn't respond to Gia's question, but instead turned his head to glance at the altar, looking for some kind of explanation. He realized that baby Serena's body was gone. It had vanished, leaving not a trace of blood nor bone behind.

While Stavros had seen nothing like what was happening, he had witnessed very disturbing things when he was trapped in Cold Currents many years ago. He had experienced Dark Magic before. And he'd felt it again tonight as Queen Zale did the bidding of the Gracious Tides.

That same darkness did not radiate off of Serena.

Whatever she was, Stavros knew she wasn't evil.

Kyle sobbed, obviously dealing with his own grief over his mother, as Moussa held him. "*Mon amour, mon amour,*" Moussa whispered, "you will be all right." He kissed Kyle all over his face and pulled him in, cradling Kyle's head on his chest.

All Moussa could think about, however, was how Serena had resurrected him—how it felt to be dead and then... *not* dead. As he held Kyle, he wondered whether this adult version of Serena retained the same powers of necromancy.

Because if she did... that could either be the biggest blessing or the most terrible curse.

18

July 28th

The sun rose over the Aegean Sea, beaming through the portholes on Gia's borrowed yacht. Sunbeams traced the edges of the room, landing on the miracle that lay next to Gia: her daughter.

Gia hadn't slept all night. Instead, she'd laid in bed next to Serena, studying her daughter's face. She looked absolutely identical to Gia's mother, Marina, in every way but one—Serena had the same golden hair that Cameron had when he was alive, instead of strawberry blonde locks like Marina.

It was so hard for Gia not to wake Serena. She had a long list of questions for her child, but she knew Serena needed sleep. They had all been through quite an ordeal, and it was going to take everyone a long time to come to terms with what had happened in the Salt Cathedral.

Gia sighed. She hovered her hand over Serena's head, wanting to stroke her hair, but instead, she carefully rolled out of bed and tiptoed up the stairs to the deck.

As she made her way to the back of the boat, she found Shadow with his feet dangling in the water. He seemed exhausted, as his broad shoulders hung low, which was unusual for him.

"It appears you did not sleep either," Gia said, bending down to take a seat next to him.

"Oof, I've a massive pain in this big loaf."

Gia only understood that he was talking about having a headache because he pointed to his head and squinted his eyes.

She smiled a little. Having Shadow around was a huge comfort. "Give me your hand."

He angled his head suspiciously. "Why?"

She didn't answer, but extended her palm and waited until he reached out to touch her.

She held his big hand in both of hers and massaged the space between his thumb and forefinger.

"My mother used to do this to me when I had a headache," she explained. "Within minutes, I would feel better."

"Wish I coulda seen that. Gia Acquaviva in her formative years." Then he winked at her. "Where'd it all go wrong, ah, love?"

She knew he was only joking, but the comment pricked her nonetheless. Gia knew that Shadow possessed all the sordid details of her life, thanks to Florent's infamous Mermaid File.

With so much private information out there about her, she felt truly naked, completely exposed.

"Do you really want to know?" she asked, licking her lips.

Shadow nodded.

She turned her gaze out to the sea as she spoke. "Everything changed for me when my mother was murdered. I... I watched it happen." Her voice trembled.

Shadow clasped his loose hand over Gia's.

"I understand," he whispered. "I understand more than you know."

They heard light footsteps behind them, and they each withdrew their hands from one another far too quickly.

Gia turned her head, and her eyes landed on a very sleepy Serena. Although she had the body of a woman, her essence remained very child-like. Serena ran to her mother and fell, scraping her knee.

"Ouch!" she yelled. Tears followed. "It hurts a lot, Mommy."

Gia opened her arms wide. "Come here, *sirenetta*. Come to your mamma."

As she embraced Serena and blew on her daughter's knee, she felt an immense peace wash over her. Losing Serena and having her back... it was almost more joy than Gia could handle. Queen Zale had robbed both Gia and Serena of Serena's childhood, and for that, Gia would be forever mournful. But she still had her baby... just in a different form.

And Gia was determined to do whatever it took to make sure that they had as many years together as they could.

She would not let the past repeat itself.

19

August 1st

"It's been thirteen days since Harper Langley was taken during the riot at OTN headquarters, and there has been no sign of her." Ashley Mason read the LION news teleprompter with extra drama.

She still hadn't forgiven Harper for firing her on live TV, but now that she was fucking Goldie Stern in exchange for rising in the ranks at LION, Ashley was really feeling herself again.

Plus, watching Harper get taken out was extremely rewarding. Heartwarming, even.

"The FBI is working diligently with OTN and with a group of Ronnie Spade supporters who have been arrested in conjunction with the riot. They are looking for any clues as to Harper Langley's whereabouts. President Spade put out a message to his supporters on Klik Klak this morning. Let's roll that."

Ashley's producer cut to a vertical video of Ronnie at his favorite wooden podium, with about sixteen flags behind him that read "Ronnie Spade for President! Again!"

"Hello, beautiful people. A big welcome to the millions of new kicky-klaky-wacky-sacky followers who have joined me on this platform. Your support means everything to me. Ronnie loves you!"

His face became somber as he moved to the meat of his speech. "I am very unhappy with what the media has been saying about my rally at the OTN offices. What has been said is very unfair and very mean! The truth is that thousands and thousands of you showed up to express your Constitutionally protected rights to free speech. But a few sicko imposters broke in and kidnapped Harper Langley. That's not your fault, and it's *certainly* not my fault. Anyway, who's to say this isn't some kind of government conspiracy, right? It's exactly the kind of black ops mission that the FBI and CIA love to do. Trust me, I know! I'm the president! You have no idea the number of crazy plans I had to kibosh. I could write an entire book about it. In fact, I think I *will* write a whole book about it. Anyway, you're great people, the best. I love you. I'll see you soon."

The studio cut back to Ashley, and she continued her coverage. "As you can see," she said, "President Spade has significantly lowered the temperature on his criticisms of the liberal media and the current administration. He's also cut back on the attacks made to the mermaid community, although anti-mermaid sentiment is still on the rise."

Behind Ashley, an image of a burning mermaid effigy appeared. "This photo was taken outside the Big Data headquarters of Bryce and Kyle Dean. The brothers are mermen and apparent heirs to their mother's mermaid colony off the coast of California. Bryce Dean is currently in custody for his alleged involvement in terrorist plots perpetrated by his mother both in Dakar, Senegal, and Venice, Italy. His younger brother, Kyle Dean, and his mother, Queen Karen, both remain at large."

"Hang around, because we'll be back with more on the Harper Langley story after the break."

20

August 1st

"I don't know what to do with Mother's body, Moussa."

Kyle sat slumped in a chair in a nondescript hotel room in Santorini. "We can't leave her at the morgue forever. I wish Bryce was here. He always knows exactly what to do in every situation."

"Come here, *mon amour,*" Moussa said.

Kyle lumbered from the chair to the bed and laid his head on Moussa's lap. He reached up and twisted one of Moussa's long locs around his finger. "I'm grateful to have you, Moussa. Seriously. Mother was always so horrible to me, but... I..." his voice trailed off as his eyes filled with tears. "I really miss her."

Moussa leaned down and kissed his lover. "*Bien sûr,* Kyle. Of course you do. After the attack in Dakar, when I thought *Maman* had been killed, I was devastated. I wanted to fall apart, really I did, but I had my people to think about. They had lost everything, and I was the only hope. The truth is, sweet boy, that no matter how grown we are, we are still our mothers' children."

Kyle closed his eyes and let thick tears fall. Moussa stroked Kyle's back as he cried.

Moussa's mind kept returning to that night on the beach when Serena had brought him back from the Great Unknown. She'd ripped him from Oumar's arms. He wondered where Karen's soul was now and whether she was at peace.

What if? Moussa wondered. *What if Serena could bring back Queen Karen, too?*

* * *

GIA'S HEART fluttered as she watched a speedboat approach the yacht. Vittore practically hung off the bow of the ship. He could not wait to get to Gia. He had been begging Stavros for days to let him go to her, but Stavros was deeply concerned about how Vittore might react when he saw Serena in her new form.

The thing was, Stavros had told Vittore the truth—but not the whole truth. He had recounted to Vittore how terrifying the battle with Queen Zale had been. He had explained that they were able to save Serena, and that she was safe and sound. However, Stavros had left out the major detail that baby Serena had been bludgeoned to death and then, somehow magically replaced by a sort of reincarnation of his niece, Marina.

So Stavros had a reason to be worried. Gia was worried, too. In fact, she had also lied to Vittore and put him off as long as possible.

"*Tesoro mio!*" Vittore called out as the speedboat approached. He waved his hands around like he was trying to stop traffic on a busy highway.

Stavros and the crew helped Vittore onto the bigger ship.

Vittore threw both arms around Gia and nearly collapsed from relief. "I love you so much, my Gia. You must promise me that from now on you will be careful. No more big risks. Yes?"

She nodded. "I promise, *Methusalamme.*"

He lifted his head and gave a huge smile. "Where is my granddaughter? All I have thought of is holding her in my lap."

Gia didn't reply. Instead, she stepped to the side, revealing Serena, who was standing behind her.

When Vittore saw her, his teeth began to chatter. He eyed the woman from top to bottom, because he recognized her. She had been his good friend. She had been the wife of his very best friend. She had been the mother of the greatest blessing of his life, Gia.

"Marina?" he asked, voice breathy as confusion set in. "Is that you?"

Serena replied, "*Nonno*, it's so good to see you again."

Gia's stomach dropped.

Vittore darted his eyes over to Gia. "What is happening, *tesoro mio*? Who is this? She looks exactly like your mamma."

Stavros placed his hands on Vittore's shoulders, because he was certain his fiancé would soon fall over from shock.

"Ah..." Gia began, having trouble finding the right words. "This is... ah... you see, when everything happened with Queen Zale... there was—"

"That is Serena!" Stavros blurted it out, because he could not stand the tension for one more second.

Vittore's eyes narrowed, as if he had become the butt of some elaborate prank.

"This is not funny," Vittore replied. "Not funny at all. Who is *this*? Some cousin? Where is my grandbaby? Stop this nonsense and bring her here *now*."

"*Nonno*," Serena insisted, "I'm right here. *I'm* Serena."

She approached him, but he tried to back away.

"Gia!" he shouted. "No! It is not right to scare an old man in this way!"

"Please, *Methusalamme*, sit down. I will explain everything."

They planted Vittore on a sofa and told him the whole story, from start to finish. He was uncharacteristically silent the entire time. When Gia and Stavros finished speaking, Vittore mulled it all over for a long time, as if deciding on a course of action.

Finally, Gia croaked, "Say something, *Methusalamme!*"

Suddenly, Vittore cried.

Gia and Stavros exchanged a worried look.

"I am so sorry, my young lover," Stavros said, hugging Vittore. "I know this is very upsetting news."

"Upsetting?!" Vittore shouted. "No! This is wonderful news! I get to see my granddaughter grow up. What man as old as I am can say the same? This is a true blessing from our Father in the Sky!"

Vittore unfolded himself and scuttled over to Serena to embrace her.

After a long while and many tears shed by all, Vittore pointed at Serena and wagged his finger. "Just because you are grown now does not mean you know everything, *sirenetta*. Listen to your *nonno*. You have much to learn. I will teach you what I know, and so will your beautiful mamma. You have many gifts, and many people will want to take them from you, so you must learn to be strong. Now, let us get you to bed, little girl, because the hour is very late."

21

August 2nd

The squeaky wheel on the bunker turned to life, waking Harper. It was pitch black outside. A circle of light bounced down the ladder as Harper's captor descended into her prison.

Harper blinked several times, and then thought, *Wait... is that a ring light? What the hell is going on?*

Harper's kidnapper threw something at her face. She patted around the cot until she found it and realized that what she was holding was a tube of lipstick.

"Make yourself up, Harper," he ordered. "I couldn't find any rouge in the medicine cabinet, so you'll have to make do. I know you're used to your fancy studio people powdering you when you go on TV."

She stared at him blankly.

"Get a move, girl! We're going live on Klik Klak in about two minutes! Slap some of that lipstick on and let's do this."

Harper was about to ask a litany of questions, but before she could speak, two of her captor's friends came clattering down into the bunker, wielding their favorite rifles.

"May I borrow your phone, sir?" she asked her captor.

He whirled around and snapped, "Do you think I'm dumb? If I give you my phone, you'll try to call the police."

"No, sir, I won't. I just can't see my face to put lipstick on. I don't have a mirror. You can hold the phone in your hands."

"Oh." He glanced over at his friends, and one tilted his head to signal his agreement. He looked back at Harper and said, "Fine."

He opened the camera app on his phone and turned it to face Harper. When she saw her face on the screen, she nearly dropped the lipstick. She barely recognized herself. Her face was sallow and puffy, hair unkempt and oily. After all, it had been weeks since she'd been outside, let alone showered.

I can't believe millions of people are going to see me looking this way. If I live through this nightmare, I better at least get a fucking book deal, she thought.

The men set her up in a chair and held a paper that they wanted her to read from. Within minutes they had logged into the app and were live on Klik Klak.

"Hi everyone," Harper began, reading from the statement her captors had prepared. "My name is Harper Langley. I want the world to know that I am safe and being treated well. The people keeping me want a few conditions to be met before releasing me. First, they want the U.S. government to stop collaborating with foreign mermaids. Second, they want an apology issued for the negative coverage of the protest at the OTN offices. And lastly, they would like the illegitimate President Bowden to make a public statement, giving his assurances that no more cooperation with mermaids will be allowed. That is all. Thank you."

She delivered the words with a monotone, unemotional affect. Inside, however, she felt hope bubbling up.

Regardless of whether these guys were using a burner phone or not, Harper knew they'd just fucked themselves. Without a doubt, the FBI would triangulate the signal and work with Klik Klak to find the location of the bunker. It was just a matter of time.

And hopefully until that day came, Harper prayed that the guns would stay pointed away from her face.

22

August 3rd

"Could we hide out in Monte Carlo?" Gia asked, throwing out suggestions to *La Nonna* and Shadow about the next phase of her life with Serena.

"*Piccolina*," La Nonna replied, "Monaco has an extradition treaty with every other developed country. If you are trying to hide from the U.S. these days, your options are quite limited. You could beg Russia for political asylum, but imagine what Putin would do to a mermaid who raises the dead." *La Nonna* paused briefly to ponder this before shaking her head and shrugging her shoulders. "I cannot imagine, actually... it exceeds my imagination. *Allora*, the other options are countries like Afghanistan and Bahrain."

Gia sighed and cursed to herself, "*Merda!*"

"I really think the best option, Gia," *La Nonna* continued, "is to call the Americans and tell them that you are ready to bring Serena if they will clear your charges and negotiate with the other governments about your crimes."

"I want time to think about it," Gia sulked.

"As you wish, *Signorina* Acquaviva."

Moussa tiptoed past Gia's quarters, "*Excusez moi,*" he said, poking his head around the door, "Kyle told me that he notified the U.S. that his mother has passed away, and the authorities let Bryce go. He's on his way back to California. Tomorrow I will fly there with Kyle for the funeral. Bryce's coronation will be the following day. It would be good if you could come."

"Who would want *me* there?" Gia replied, confused.

"Gia, think about it. The conflicts started because *Maman* sided with you. If you can show everyone that you have moved on and forgiven Queen Karen, I think that such a diplomatic gesture would go a long way toward healing Pan Atargatic relations."

"You expect *me* to be the peacemaker, King Moussa? After everything that happened?"

"Do you think it's easy for *me*, Gia?" Moussa snapped. "Consider the genocide. Consider Oumar. I've lost so much because of you. Therefore, I *demand* you come to the funeral. Think of it as a way to repay your debt to me."

Gia winced as she thought of Oumar. Moussa had her right in her soft spot by mentioning his dead husband, so there was no escaping. "*Bene*, yes," Gia conceded, "Moussa I will go to California with you." Then she glanced over to *La Nonna*. "Call General Thomas and tell him to come to pick us up in California after the funeral. Serena and I will go to D.C. and face what we must."

ONCE THE BUSINESS of the day was done and *La Nonna* had gone, Gia welcomed Serena into the room.

"How was your time with Vittore?" Gia asked.

"He's hilarious, Mommy. I really love him."

Gia grinned. "I know."

Gia patted the bed beside her, and Serena plopped down on it, lowering her head onto Gia's shoulder.

"Serena, tomorrow we will go to America. There is so much I must te—"

"America?!" Serena squealed. "Are we going to see my grandparents? I miss them. I know Grandmother Brownie will be so happy to see me. And maybe Grandpa Royce will be less grumpy with me now that I'm all grown up."

Gia's smile dropped. "Serena, I am very sorry to tell you this... but... your father's parents, the Langleys... they are no longer with us."

"What does that mean?"

"They died, *sirenetta,* I am so sorry."

"*Died?!*" Serena cried. "No, Mommy! That's not fair. I barely got to spend any time with them. Why didn't you tell me?"

"I do not understand how all of this works, Serena. You seem to remember so much... to know so much, but it seems that there are some limits as to what you understand. I had spoken of the Langleys, when you were still a baby, but perhaps you did not understand what happened to them until now."

"So..." Serena's eyes glazed over while she was trying to make sense of it all. "I'll never see them ever again?"

"No, *sirenetta,* not in this life, *amore.*"

"That's horrible!"

"I am so sorry. Give me a hug."

Serena came close to Gia, but then shoved her away. "Are you going to die, too?"

Gia put her hand under Serena's chin and lifted it. "Not for a long, long time."

"Good," Serena huffed, "because I need you. Children need their mommies."

Gia's heart ached hearing Serena say that, because she knew it was true. How different would her life have been had her own mother lived?

23

August 3rd

Ashley Mason could have died and gone to heaven. Not only was she the new golden girl at LION, but she now had Harper's mermaid bestie in the studio.

"Queen Mother Awa Diop of Senegal," Ashely said, greeting her guest for the evening. "You've been making quite a stir around the country, haven't you?"

"Thanks to you and this..." Awa paused, glancing around the studio with disdain, "this sad little disinformation factory, I have received a large number of death threats, Miss Mason. So, apparently I *am* stirring up a bit of controversy."

Ashley Mason fluttered her eyelashes, trying to disarm Awa. "Speaking of controversy, the relationship that you have with Harper Langley has been a big focus of attention. I know you're a... lord, what is it you call it these days? I hate to upset the LMNOP crowd... you're a *lesbian*, right? And is Harper Langley your lover? Are y'all sleeping together, and if so, who's the man in the relationship?"

Awa remained utterly unphased. She replied without the slightest hint of resentment. "I have been happily married for over a century to the same beautiful woman, Queen Consort Mariama Diop."

But Ashley pressed on. "There have been a lot of rumors," Ashley replied, tossing her hands up. "You know I had to ask!"

Awa shrugged.

"So," Ashley continued, "what is it that you wanted to tell America tonight?"

"I am gravely concerned about Harper's safety. And after that hostage video went viral on Klik Klak yesterday, I thought that it was of supreme importance that I support my friend and publicly call on President Bowden to pressure the authorities to find—"

A little red buzzer on the desk went off next to Ashley.

"Oh!" Ashley shouted. "That's our breaking news buzzer. I'm gonna have to cut you off, Queen Awa."

Ashley readjusted her earpiece and then said, "President Ronnie Spade is hosting an impromptu press conference, and he says he has news about Harper Langley. We're going to patch into that feed. We are now going live to Ronnie Spade."

Ashley Mason's face was replaced with Ronnie Spade's ruddy mug. He tried to smile, but only managed to make the muscles in his face appear as though he was having a bowel movement.

"Hello, hi, good to see all of you beautiful people here in the briefing room. Well, not you, Spencer," he said, pointing to a red-headed reporter in the back of the room. "You're very unfair, very rude to me. You don't like me very much, and I don't like you. Can someone please take Spencer out? Okay, wonderful. Thanks a lot."

Ronnie finally stopped his typical ad libbing and got to the point. "My campaign has been in contact with some very good people, and unlike the police and the FBI and all the other ding-a-lings working this case, my people and I have actually had a breakthrough. We know where Harper Langley is, and we are now negotiating for her release. I will have more information tomorrow."

And with that, Blonde Wig left the room, answering no questions and giving no further details.

The studio cut back over to Ashley Mason.

"Breaking news indeed," Ashley mumbled, mustering as much enthusiasm as she could. She was rather hoping that Harper wouldn't return from this little adventure.

Ashley turned to Queen Awa, "What is your take on what we just saw?"

"I am very eager for my friend to return home," Awa replied. Then she glared at the camera lens and said, "And she better return home *unharmed*."

24

August 4th

The yacht was rocking in the current, and Gia laid awake, observing Serena. She edged out of the bed and moved to the door of the stateroom, leaving it to hobble down the hallway. The fracture was improving, but it would still take time to heal completely.

On her way to the wet bar, she bumped into Shadow.

"Thought I might tumble down the kitchen sink," he said, smiling. "Want one?"

"Real English, please," Gia replied, narrowing her eyes playfully.

He pointed at her. "Bourbon, rocks... the cheap shit."

She folded her hands like she was praying and said, "*Per favore*, I will love you forever."

They sat close to one another, each drinking their whiskeys, hers on the rocks, his neat.

Shadow shifted in his seat. "It's our last night together for a while, ain't it?"

"So it seems." Gia picked a piece of ice out of her glass and sucked on it.

Shadow parted his lips to speak but stopped himself. That happened two or three times, but then he cleared his throat and gulped his drink.

Finally Gia broke the silence.

"I want to say thank you, Shadow. These last few months... you have been... I have come to rely on you so much. You have gone above and beyond your duties. I am not an easy client, I know."

Shadow bit the inside of his cheek while she spoke. He didn't like being reminded he was merely her employee.

"Yeah," he said, "but now you're movin' onto bigger and better things. Right? Maybe they'll assign you a couple Secret Service agents," he smiled.

Gia considered his words. She really didn't want anyone keeping watch over her. Except Shadow, of course. That realization struck her hard, and she felt sad. However, she masked this truth as best as she could.

"I prefer to look after myself," she said flatly.

He let out a chuckle. "Ha! Don't I know all about that? Oh, yes, I do."

"I will miss you, Shadow," Gia admitted.

"I'll still be working for you, just not so close and personal."

Gia cast her eyes down. "I wish you could come with me to America."

He blew a raspberry. "Nah, no tellin' what Uncle Sam would do if he got his hands round the likes of me. I may have one or two... misunderstandings... still active over there. Don't you worry, love. I'll still be knocking skulls for you over here. Trying to sort things on the business side."

"I wonder," Gia asked, suddenly feeling shaky and vulnerable, "what do you *really* think of me?"

A smile danced in his eyes.

"I think you're the biggest baddie there ever was."

It was Gia's turn to chuckle now. "A baddie? What is that?"

"You're a bad bitch, Gia!"

"I am," she laughed. Then she lowered her voice to a raspy whisper. "I am *very* bad indeed."

"I understand you," Shadow replied, matching her tone and dropping his own volume. "I'm as bad as they come."

He was much closer to her now; they were only inches apart.

She was watching his lips, those thick lips that she longed to kiss. He knew she wanted him, and he wanted her, too, but he held back.

And then Shadow broke the trance.

"You have a long flight tomorrow, Gia. You should get some sleep."

Gia found herself disappointed by his dismissal, which left her nearly panting. She wasn't used to having someone else call the shots.

"Ah," she replied. "It *is* quite late. Will I see you in the morning, then?"

"Nah, gonna slip out soon."

"Oh, I see." His words stung her.

Would he have even said goodbye to me? Gia wondered.

She lingered close to him for a moment longer.

"Good night, Gia."

With a slight sigh that she tried to keep to herself, she turned around to head to her room.

"Good night, Shadow," she called out as she left, feeling resigned and discouraged. But as she turned the corner, she heard quick footsteps come up behind her.

Shadow put his hand on her shoulder and spun her around.

They were face to face. He whispered, "I can't let you leave like that, can I, love?"

He wrapped his arms around her waist and dipped her backward, kissing her deeply one time.

"And that'll have to hold you over," he said firmly.

He gave her a pat on the butt and walked away from her, heading down the hall into the darkness. And Gia was left breathless and wanting.

* * *

KYLE PLACED his hands on his mother's coffin as the crew at the Santorini airport loaded her body into the cargo hold of the company jet. Moussa was there with him, standing by him. They boarded the plane together, holding hands.

Gia ascended the airstairs with Serena. Vittore and Stavros followed closely behind.

As they flew away, Gia stared out the window. She thought back to the first time that Cameron came aboard her plane. He watched everything on the ground get smaller and smaller.

She leaned over to Serena and said, "Once your father told me that he loved how small everything looks from the sky. It reminded him of a train set he had as a child, and he created a town with tracks in the woods and let the train loop around and around."

"What happened to my dad?" Serena asked, her expression curious and childlike.

Gia's heart thumped in her chest. She realized she was going to have to have a lot of uncomfortable conversations with Serena. What would her daughter think of everything in Florent's Mermaid File? Would Serena reject her when she found out what kind of monster she really was?

She began to speak, but Vittore wobbled over, having overheard the question. He inserted himself in the conversation, as he was known to do.

"*Sirenetta mia*, when you have lived as long as I have, you understand that it matters less how a man dies than how he lived his life. After all, what is death? Hopefully a few moments, nothing more. Maybe weeks or months for the unlucky. I can tell you this, Serena, your papa loved your mamma, and he wanted to share his life with her, and with you. Do not dwell so on the morbidity of the end. Enjoy the wonders of this life... make friends, fall in love, be generous with your heart. That is life."

Serena hugged Vittore and kissed him on the cheek. "I love you, *Nonno*."

He melted, and his heart filled with so much joy he was sure he would burst.

* * *

THE CALIFORNIANS GREETED the funeral procession with careful mourning and measured tears. Karen's coffin was paraded through the open industrial space and laid on an altar made from a reclaimed airplane wing.

The Dean brothers—the princes—received their people one by one. There were delegates from all the Pan Atargatic nations, the usual suspects. But also in attendance was Togashi. People stared at the reclusive Archivist, whom they had heard about for many years but never seen.

The entire place was nearly silent, so even the slightest sound reverberated around the smooth concrete walls of the hydroelectric plant that housed the colony.

Moussa buzzed with anxious energy. He had a plan, and while he was not sure if it would work, he felt compelled to try to execute it, nonetheless.

He pulled Serena and Gia from the procession line and scurried them over to another area, a closed off room where they could speak in private.

"Serena," Moussa said, his eyes full of mischief, "we need your help. You brought me back from the Great Unknown. I want you to raise Queen Karen as well."

"Are you crazy?" Gia shouted, turning on him.

"Shh!" Moussa hissed. "Kyle is a mess. He watched his mother die a violent death in front of his eyes. Do you know how much that will fuck up a person?"

I know better than anyone, Gia thought.

"King Moussa," Gia chided, "why would you seek to revive your enemy, *our* enemy?"

"Gia, my mother told me last night that the Ice Folk are mounting a huge offensive. When she went to the Arctic Circle, she said she saw them training and preparing all kinds of weapons. She spoke to the leaders a few days ago, and they are ready to attack. If we don't stop this war, I think they will wipe out all the merfolk in California and

New Zealand. You being here at the funeral has helped put people at ease, making them think we are headed toward peace... but without Queen Karen around, I don't think Bryce and Kyle stand a chance against the Ice Folk. Is she my enemy? Yes. But for the sake of saving more of our kind, I am willing to put aside my own hatred."

Gia shook her head. "No, we do not understand how Serena's power works. What if bringing Karen back kills her?"

"Come on, Gia!" Moussa snapped. "She brought me back to life when she was only a baby! She is a grown woman now. Surely her powers are even stronger."

"I do not—"

"I'll do it!" Serena blurted out in reply.

"Serena," Gia said through gritted teeth, "I forbid you."

"Mommy, you can't protect me from myself. I want to try. You heard Moussa... if this war escalates, then who knows where it will stop?"

Moussa took Serena by the hand and snuck her out of the room, behind the crowd, to the back of Karen's coffin.

"How does it work, your power?" Moussa asked, whispering.

"I don't know," Serena answered. "I only ever did it that one time with you... and I didn't know what would happen."

"Do you need to touch her?"

"Maybe?"

"*Merde*," Moussa cursed. "Here's what we will do. I will go make a speech and draw everyone's attention to the opposite side of the room. When I do that, make your way to the front of the casket, open it, and do your magic."

Serena nodded.

Moussa bolted to the other end of the large room and clapped his hands. "Attention! Attention, everyone! I am King Moussa of Senegal."

Awa and Mariama glanced up from the procession line, looking rather cross. A speech at a time like this was highly improper.

Moussa continued, "Queen Karen of California was a strong leader who reigned for..."

He droned on, and Serena tuned him out, focusing herself on what needed to be done. Gia shuffled over to Serena.

"Stop this!" she whispered.

"Mommy," Serena pleaded, "you have to let me try. Please, go."

Serena lifted the lid of the coffin and gazed down upon Karen's sunken cheeks. She closed her eyes and lowered her hands into the casket, touching Karen's face.

There was a warm sensation growing inside Serena. She could feel electricity in her chest.

But could she harness it?

25

August 4th

"Use more glue this time!" The former President barked as his stylist teased his blonde wig piece. "Do you know that some Internet troll made a meme of me with my hair blowing off? I won't have that! Especially not today!"

Ronnie peeled back the curtain inside the tour bus and glanced around the yard of the rural Alabama farm where he was parked. His camera crew and re-election staff were coordinating with the local sheriff. The police department was on hand, eager for their time in the glowing spotlight of their idol, Ronnie Spade.

A producer knocked on the door of the tour bus, and Ronnie's chief of staff answered it. "We're live in three minutes," the producer warned.

"Got it," said the chief of staff. "I'll have the president out in two."

Fluffed and puffed, Ronnie was ready to face the camera. He took his mark at the edge of the farm and the camera recorded him waddling to his podium.

"Good morning, beautiful people. Thank you so much for joining me here on this fine day in Alabama. I am coming to you with the best news. I always do that, don't I? I have the best news, always. The media doesn't like to admit it, but I'm a big draw, the biggest ever, everyone says so. I get the networks their ratings, but do they thank me? Oh, no! Never, never. They're always trying to catch me doing something bad. I'm a good guy, okay? And you can't keep a good guy down."

The camera panned across a line of police officers nodding and cracking up. They loved Ronnie's schtick.

"As usual, I broke the Internet the other day with news that I had a lead on the location of Harper Langley. I break the Internet so often that it's a wonder the whole thing's still running. I have more Klik Klak followers than anyone, but you know what they do? They take them away. I beat Kim Kardashian by millions and millions. Anyway, moving on! We have found Harper, and it's all thanks to some excellent police work by this fine man over here. Turn the camera and show everyone the sheriff."

The camera tilted to the left and then back to Ronnie Spade.

"Thanks to him and to me, we know exactly where Harper Langley is! She is right underneath me."

Ronnie took a moment to let that dramatic revelation land.

Then he said, "We're going to rescue her right now, live on camera."

The camera swung around and followed him for a little while as he walked behind the farmhouse. A few police officers lifted a camouflage tarp off the ground, revealing a hatch with a wheel.

"She's in here," Ronnie said. "Open the bunker."

The sheriff twisted the wheel, and stepped back. Ronnie lifted the door and sat it upright on its hinges. Then he called out to Harper.

"Harper Langley! It's Ronnie Spade! We're here to rescue you! You can come out now! You're safe, Harper. Thanks to me, you're safe! Don't forget to thank me for saving your life!"

The camera pushed into the bunker, lighting the space up. Harper raised her hands above her face, blocking the light. She stumbled toward the door. Two police officers climbed down the ladder and helped lift her out, placing her on the grass above.

Cheers rang out as Harper stood in the sunlight for the first time in weeks. It was a scorching Alabama day, and she felt lightheaded.

The camera was still on her. Ronnie Spade approached her, extending his hand to shake hers.

"How do you feel, Harper?" he asked, with an ear-to-ear grin.

Harper blinked a few times and swayed. She lost her footing and her knees gave out. Ronnie rushed behind her to catch her, but they both fell backward, onto the ground. Everyone scrambled to help them up. Ronnie stood up slowly, wiping dirt and grass from his suit.

"Bring a stretcher for Harper!" Ronnie yelled.

Every second of action was recorded as Harper was laid onto the stretcher, given water, and tucked into the back of an ambulance.

The camera once again turned to Ronnie.

"That's not all, folks! What did I tell you? I said I have the *best* news. We also have here the individuals who perpetrated this crime. Bring them out, please."

The sheriff and his police force carted out seven men and plunked them in front of Ronnie.

Ronnie approached the leader, the man who had been in charge of watching over Harper.

"Why did you do this?" Ronnie asked.

"Mr. President, sir, we... uh... we acted on our own without any direction from you or your campaign... or... uh... any other individuals connected to you now or in the future."

Clearly, the man had been coached by Ronnie's massive team of lawyers.

Ronnie stared down the camera lens. "You heard that. No matter what the lying media says, I am not responsible for this heinous crime."

The seven detainees all cried out, "We love you Ronnie! We're sorry! We love you!"

Ronnie smiled and pointed at the camera.

"That's all for today!"

And then they cut the feed.

26

August 4th

Serena concentrated and drew the buzzing energy in her chest down into her arms and then to her hands, trying to establish her control over it. Her fingers glowed with golden light and became transparent at the tips. The same glow spread to Queen Karen, illuminating her body. Within seconds, the intensity of the light was so bright that the beams attracted the attention of the room, and everyone turned to face Serena.

Serena took several steps backward, and as she did, a long, golden string formed between her hands and Karen's head. That cord snatched Karen up, and her body sat upright in its coffin. Serena lifted both arms, and Karen's body replicated the motion, lifting the bottom half of the coffin. Zombie Karen swung her tail out of the coffin, and it tipped over. Her body tumbled off the altar and onto the floor.

The mourners shrieked and gasped in horror as their queen's tail split into two legs and she went scuttling across the floor on all fours. Serena swung her arms in a big circle with great force, and Karen rose to her feet.

Serena balled her hands into fists and then released them with a flick.

Queen Karen's eyelids opened.

The same glowing light Serena emanated was now projected from Karen's eyes. Karen cocked her head to an unnatural angle, and there was a snapping sound, as her bones popped into place one by one, reanimated. There was a hole in Karen's chest right where her heart should have been, and light seeped through it. They all watched the hole close up, and then Karen let out a guttural wail that sent everyone running.

She was alive.

An invisible force stretched Karen's body tall and long.

Queen Karen spun around to face Serena and with a scratchy, shrill voice demanded, "WHAT HAVE YOU DONE TO ME, CHILE'?"

27

August 8th

Queen Awa and Mariama met Harper at Teterboro Airport in New Jersey. They arranged for Harper's driver to wait for her on the tarmac, and as soon as Harper descended the airsteps, Awa ushered her into the car. When they were in and the doors were closed, Awa wrapped her arms around Harper.

Harper allowed herself to be comforted by the women. She had been through a horrible experience, and her focus, up to this moment, had been simply on surviving. Now Harper had to face her trauma, and Awa knew Harper needed a friend to support her.

"It's all right, Harper. We have you, and everything is going to be much better from now on. Let's get you home."

* * *

MARIAMA ASKED the staff at Langley Manor to set up Bronwyn's old office for the three women. Rightly so, she had foreseen that Harper would need a smaller space to recover, something cozy.

What Mariama had not considered was how the small cottage would trigger Harper's guilt over her decision to assassinate her parents. Harper had a host of complicated emotions she needed to face.

But first: gossip... and cocktails.

Awa flipped the switch on what looked like a slurpee machine, and the thing came whirring to life. "Talia Levy sent over this Frosé maker."

"How thoughtful," Harper joked.

Awa laughed. "You know Talia loves anything pink!"

"Queen," Harper leveled her gaze at Awa, blowing her a kiss across the room, "thank you so much for being here with me. You too, Mariama."

"I wouldn't dare leave you alone, Harper," Awa chided.

"Now, please tell me what has been happening since I've been gone."

Awa and Mariama glanced at each other and shared a big sigh. And Awa went for it.

"An evil queen attempted to sacrifice your niece to the multi-God whom we all worshiped... but apparently that god is also evil. She did not exactly succeed in her sacrifice, but Serena is now a fully grown adult. Queen Karen died trying to protect Serena... but at Karen's funeral a few days ago, Serena raised her from the dead. Karen is very pissed off about being back in the world of the living. I think that covers it, but I may be missing some details."

Harper shook her head, confused and unable to take it all in. "Is that Frosé ready yet?"

Awa pulled the handle down and filled a margarita glass with the sweet, frozen booze. She handed it to Harper who took a big gulp.

"Ow!" Harper yelled. "Brain freeze! Jesus!"

She massaged her temples and said, "I need you to explain everything from the start... and in vivid detail, please. But first... Serena... you said Serena is *grown*?"

"Mmhmm."

"How is that possible?"

"Apparently, it's the power of ancient goddesses who were long lost to history."

Harper laughed breathily, more out of nerves than finding anything funny.

"Wow," she said, finally. "I hate babies... so maybe this is good?"

Awa shrugged.

Harper returned to nursing her glass, taking smaller sips this time. "What's happening with Queen Karen now? Is she *alive* alive *a la* Jon Snow?"

Awa scrunched her eyebrows together, trying to place the name. "Jon Snow? Who is that?"

Harper laughed again, this time genuinely. "Do they not have HBO underwater? He's the lead character in an epic fantasy show. Anyway... let's start at the beginning, please."

Awa and Mariama clinked their glasses to Harper's, and Awa winked at Harper. "It's so good to have you home, Blondie."

28

August 20th

The sleeping quarters at the Pentagon didn't feel exactly like being in jail, but the accommodations were austere enough that they gave Gia flashbacks. She and Serena had been smuggled into the infamous building with zero fanfare. In fact, out of deference to Gia, Awa had been so tight-lipped about Gia's deal with General Thomas that, so far, nothing had leaked to the media.

Their days consisted of interviews and tests, from sunrise to sundown—not that they could tell what time of day it was in their forgotten basement wing of the building. Gia stayed by Serena's side the entire time. So far, the officials were frustrated. They had not had luck in accessing Serena's powers, nor could they glean any considerable understanding of their origins. There were no golden light explosions.

The experts had become more and more niche. After exhausting even the roster of approved psychics, General Thomas finally threw his hands up and asked Gia what she thought.

"Bring Togashi, the Archivist," Gia had suggested.

And so, on their sixteenth day at the Pentagon, Gia and Serena were formally introduced to Togashi.

"It was very impressive to see you using magic so intuitively at Karen's funeral," Togashi said to Serena.

Serena bit her lip. "I don't know what I'm doing."

"This is why I am here," Togashi explained. "To study you and, at last, pierce the veil between this world and the Great Unknown."

General Thomas watched them from behind a two-way mirror. He pressed a button and spoke into a microphone, airing his voice over a loudspeaker to Togashi and Serena.

"I would like to remind you, as you begin on your magic... uh... *journey*, that you may not leave the premises or in any way harm or damage persons or property. Should you violate the terms of this agreement, Gia Acquaviva will immediately be remitted to the custody of the Italian government, where she will no doubt, be prosecuted for her crimes. Thank you. Please continue."

Gia sat next to General Thomas behind the glass. He glanced over at her and flashed a fake, closed-lip smile.

Togashi asked Serena to sit in a chair. Togashi removed a crystal wand from a leather bag and circled her, tracing her head with the wand over and over.

"Close your eyes," Togashi said. She did. "Listen to the sound of my voice and follow my instructions. In your mind's eye you see a blackish-red haze. It pulsates with flashes of yellow. Those flashes look like veins. Grab onto one of those veins as if it is a rope. Pull yourself to the top of the rope. Sit on it. Now you realize that it is actually a train, and that this train is headed up toward the sky, beyond the sky. Now you are inside the train. There are other passengers there, riding alongside you. Observe who they are. Study the landscape outside the window of the train. Now I will ask you some questions. Who is sitting beside you?"

Serena's head bobbed strangely, as though the metaphorical train she was riding was real and hitting a patch of rough track. "My grandmother, Marina. Marina Galanis."

Togashi nodded. "Talk to her. Ask her questions. What does she say?"

Serena's mouth moved as though she was talking, but no words came out.

"Marina?" Togashi asked. "What do you wish to say? Do you have a message?"

Serena's mannerisms changed, and she spoke in Greek. "*Koúkla mou*," she said.

The hairs on Gia's neck stood on end. The sound of her mother's voice nearly brought her to tears.

"Gia, my daughter, you have suffered too long because of what happened to me. You have hurt people, killed people, and you have caused damage to families... your pain will echo across generations. You must heal yourself, Gia, please. I love you, and I wish that I had been given the time to watch over you and guide you. I am inside Serena, *koúkla mou*, always watching you. Know that."

Gia was weeping silently, and she wanted her mother to appear in real life to embrace her, but all she saw was Serena, quietly perched on a chair.

Togashi tapped lightly with the crystal wand on the space between Serena's eyebrows. "Serena, what do you see around you? What is outside?"

Serena spoke again, this time with her own voice. "We are floating on a river now. Everything is so beautiful outside. I think the train is stopping, and I would like to get off and walk around."

"No, child, the lands beyond the train are not meant for you. Stay on board. Tell me, who is there with you now?"

With her eyes still closed, Serena moved her head, as if studying other passengers.

"Daddy's here with me... and Florent... and someone named Pierre. They just got on the train at the last stop."

Serena laughed and laughed as though someone was telling her jokes.

That must be Cameron, Gia thought.

When Serena started humming, Gia's suspicions were confirmed.

Serena was definitely talking to Cameron. After all, he always had a song on his lips—even though it drove Gia crazy.

What a shame that they cannot share moments like this. They are very much alike, Serena and Cameron.

Serena spoke again. "Mommy, they all say that they spoke to Marina, and they understand what happened to you. They aren't angry with you anymore about the things you have done, and they want you to be happy. That's the most important thing... they want you to find love and stop hurting people. They're begging you, Mommy."

A scream or a whimper—something was caught in Gia's throat and she wanted to scratch it out. Everyone in the observation room was looking at her. She had tears streaming down her face, and she wished she could disappear.

On the other side of the glass, Serena stood up, eyes still closed, and walked over to the mirror. She tapped on it with her finger.

"Are you listening, Mommy? They're all here with me now. They're all bleeding. They want you to make it stop."

29

August 21st

Queen Karen felt like a hostage in her own half-rotted body. Her death had been horrible and painful, but the afterlife made up for all of that. Feeling the limitless expanse of the Great Unknown was liberating. She was everywhere and nowhere at once, and there were many universes to explore. She was just getting started.

But then Serena yanked her back and locked her in a body that no longer fit, nor functioned as it once did.

Karen had not taken to reanimation like Moussa had. Coming back to life had not given her a sense of equanimity. In fact, she was livid, raging even.

And she was determined to stop Serena from doing this to anyone else.

Karen had pried very sensitive intel out of Kyle, and she knew exactly with whom she most wanted to share those powerful secrets: President Ronnie Spade.

* * *

"HELLO BEAUTIFUL PEOPLE," Ronnie Spade said, speaking to his followers on Klik Klak Live. "One important thing to know about me is that when they zig, I zag. The lying media says I hate mermaids. I call bullcrap on that. I've never said a bad word about mermaids. Never! That's why, today, I have an important announcement to make. I have a special guest joining me on the Wacky-Quacky app. Okay, let's plug her in!"

He pressed a button, and the screen split in two. Queen Karen appeared on the other side.

"This is Queen Karen, the ruler of California. Not *all* of California, obviously. *Unfortunately!* I wish Karen was in charge of California. She's a lifelong Republican, and she has been a very generous donor to my campaign. Haven't you, Queen Karen?"

"Indeed, Ronnie," Karen replied, grinning. "You're the real deal. I still think it's a travesty that you're not in the White House right now."

Ronnie's face went red, but he shook it off and stayed on message. "Everyone, my big news for you today is that I have appointed Queen Karen Dean as a Special Advisor on Mermaid/Human relations. We will be working very closely together. I know that the FBI... I like to call them the Fool's Bureau of Idiots... they have been working with the other crooked organization, the Department of Justice, to try to pin crimes on Karen that are absolutely untrue. We will not only clear Queen Karen's name, but we will do big things together, huge! Like solving climate change. Suck on that, Alexandria Ocasio-Cortez. And Karen also has something really important to tell you. Go on, Karen, talk."

Karen clenched her jaw. "The criminal mastermind, Gia Acquaviva, has gotten her hands on Ancient Magic. She and her daughter are now using it to raise people from the dead. How do I know this? Because they brought me back to life! I was blissing out in heaven, and now I am back here in this shithole country, trapped in this rotting meat sack that's a sad excuse for a body. America needs us to save it from these evil women. If they brought me back to life, can you imagine what the liberals will do once they have that power? There will never be a fair election again. They're gonna look at the voter roles and resurrect every goddamn left-leaning body in the graveyard and force them to Vote Blue. I don't know about you, but that scares the living shit out of me."

Ronnie nodded in agreement. "It's a horror show. And what else, Karen? Tell them the other thing."

Karen took her cue. "Gia Acquaviva and her body-snatching daughter are in the Pentagon *right now* with our corrupt generals."

"Disgusting!" Ronnie shouted.

Karen raised a fist into the air. "We have to stop them before it's too late!"

30

August 22nd

It was a balmy morning in Arlington, Virginia. At Marymount University, near the Pentagon, students moved into housing. A sophomore stapled flyers to trees, seeking volunteers to train service animals that would eventually visit hospice centers to cheer up cancer patients.

Along the roads and highways near the Pentagon, fifteen large moving trucks clattered along. Anyone would have assumed those trucks were filled with the belongings of college students or newly-weds moving into their first house or retirees setting out on adventures in their golden years.

The truth, however, was much more sinister. Each and every truck was filled to the brim with ammonal—a highly explosive mix of ammonium nitrate and aluminum powder.

The militia group driving the trucks toward the Pentagon had a clear mission.

They had studied the 9/11 attack and gleaned important insights. Whereas the plane crash had largely affected only one section of the building, the truck drivers today would split into groups, so that the explosives would encircle all five points of the Pentagon.

They hoped to do much more damage than was done on 9/11. Their goal was to crater the whole building.

In a coordinated effort, at two minutes past nine o'clock in the morning, the drivers busted through the checkpoints all around the Pentagon and lit their respective fuses. The explosion was so strong that it was felt more than seven miles away at Marymount. The ground shook so violently that it brought several students to their knees.

The militia's homemade bombs brought down the walls of the Pentagon, shattering the windows and crumbling the concrete. Because of the design of the building, large parts of it withstood the initial impact, but fell later like dominos. The destruction continued for over an hour.

General Thomas was attending a meeting in the Oval Office when the attack happened. President Bowden was evacuated to a secure and secret location, along with senior officials all over Washington. However, General Thomas insisted on immediately traveling to the Pentagon.

After all, the people in that building were under his chain of command. He needed to be there to lead them—and to count the dead.

31

August 25th

For the last day, Gia and Serena had been trying to dig their way out of the Pentagon's basement. The women explored the area for any openings and tried to follow them, to see if they led to the outside world. They couldn't find Togashi and didn't know if he had been killed in one of the blasts. However, finding him was a secondary priority; the first was getting to safety.

When the women had explored every available direction, only to be met with a dead end, they realized the only thing that they could do was sit and wait to be discovered. They hoped they would be, at least—and before it was too late.

Gia wished at that moment that she had magical abilities. She imagined filling the space around them with water and easily moving stray office chairs, concrete blocks, and steel beams from their path. But she had no such power, so all she could do was keep moving shit around, yelling for help, and comforting Serena.

In the darkness, Gia held her daughter and told her stories about her own life, about Cameron, about Vittore.

"It is strange, Serena," Gia explained, "because I feel as though it has been so long since all these things happened, but it is a trick, you see. I lost time with you. It is as though we snipped a whole portion out of a film. In a way, things do not make sense. I feel so old all of a sudden, because you are an adult now."

"I understand, Mommy."

They listened to the sound of people dying all around them. On the other side of some rubble, a man had been shrieking for hours and now only had the strength to whimper. Serena instinctively knew he would be gone soon.

She closed her eyes and practiced all that Togashi had taught her. Soon she was riding the train to the Great Unknown. It was packed with people from the Pentagon. They were confused and bloody. Serena explained what was happening to them and where they were headed. No one seemed to know the source of the explosion. She told them not to worry about that now—that none of it mattered anymore, because they were about to experience the most wonderful adventure just as soon as the train stopped.

"Aren't you coming?" asked one woman as the train doors slid open.

Serena shook her head. "Not today."

"If you see my father, will you tell him I love him and that I'll be waiting for him... and for Mom, too?"

"Yes, of course I will. What is your father's name?

"General George Thomas."

Serena's heart thumped in her chest and her words got caught in her throat. She realized that whatever had happened to cause the explosion at the Pentagon was going to be very personal to General Thomas. He was probably looking for his daughter right now, not realizing she was already dead.

"General Thomas," Serena said, finally. "I know him. I will tell him I saw you, and that you're going to be all right."

The woman left the train, and the doors closed. Serena opened her eyes and started to cry. Gia held her daughter close to her heart and stroked her hair.

"Shhh, *sirenetta*," Gia said, "they will find us soon."

32

August 26th

When the concrete slabs that held Gia and Serena underground were finally lifted, and they saw the sunshine again, they threw their arms around each other and wept. Serena knew what to expect in the afterlife, so she was not afraid of death, but she was so eager to live and to experience life on this plane.

However, the devastation around them was difficult to take in—even for someone as experienced in gore as Gia. She had never seen bodies blown to pieces. This looked like a war zone.

Serena and Gia were given first aid, food, and water. Then, they waited in a protected area under a makeshift shelter, because they were high-profile assets. A few hours later, General Thomas came to see them.

"A militia group has taken responsibility for the attack," he explained. "They are threatening more attacks unless we stop working with mermaids. The good thing is that they don't know that you're both alive. We've been briefed that a major objective of the group was to eliminate both of you. You're under our protection, and we will move you to a safe house soon."

"General," Gia replied, "we were *already* under your protection, and this happened. The Pentagon is supposed to be one of the safest buildings in the world. I am not sure you really can keep us safe."

He was tired, and his face hung in a defeated shape. "We're doing the best we can under the circumstances, Miss Acquaviva."

Serena spoke before Gia could get another word in. "General Thomas, I saw your daughter."

His eyes went watery. "My daughter... she's gone. We found her body this morning."

Serena nodded. "I spoke to her last night. She was on her way to the Great Unknown. She was happy, General Thomas, really. She said she loves you and that she'll be waiting over there for you and for her mom."

The general burst into tears and had to hold the back of a chair to keep from falling down. He realized in that moment that he had been in shock, and the reality of the situation was becoming clear. This was real. His daughter was gone.

He sobbed for a few minutes but finally pulled himself together.

He swallowed his tears and faced Serena. "I want you..." it was hard for him to speak without crying. "I want you to bring her back, Serena."

Serena's eyes shot over to Gia's. They were wide with panic. Serena knew for certain that the general's daughter did not want to come back, and furthermore, she had no idea what the condition of her body was.

"I don't—"

"We're going to her!" he cried, pulling Serena up by her arm.

"Do not touch her like that!" Gia screamed, slapping the general's hand and trying to pry it off Serena.

He let go of Serena, but he turned on his heel and came face to face with Gia. He bore down on her and screamed at her, barely an inch from her face. "If you were me right now, and my daughter had the power to bring Serena back to life, you know good goddamn well that you would do exactly what I'm about to do. So, shut the hell up and get in line, Acquaviva!"

Gia was shocked into silence. He was absolutely right, though. If there was any chance of saving Serena in a similar circumstance, she would have done anything.

"*Bene*," she conceded, "Serena, come, we will go with the general."

He shielded them as they went from tent to tent, finally arriving at one place where they were laying out the dead.

The general's daughter was missing an arm and half her face.

"Go on," he insisted. "Do the thing."

Serena shook her head. "I can't."

"What do you mean you can't?" he yelled.

"I don't think she wants to come back like that." Serena pointed to the woman's mangled head.

"How would you know?" he insisted.

"I promise you, General," Serena pleaded. "Your daughter looked good over there. She was happy. She is at peace. I can't bring her back to suffer. Please, I beg you. Don't make me do this."

"Do it right now, or your mother goes to jail!"

Serena's eyes welled up with tears. "Mommy?" She looked to Gia for help.

"Do not worry about me, Serena. Do what you feel is right."

Serena closed her eyes and wept. The general had given her an impossible choice. She didn't want to lose her mother, so she gave in. "What's your daughter's name?"

"Zawade," he replied, barely able to breathe.

Serena closed her eyes. She reached down and wrapped her hand around Zawade's and focused, as Togashi had taught her. She remembered the stop where the Zawade had exited the train. Serena went back there in her mind. The train doors opened, and she called out for Zawade.

No one came.

"Zawade! Zawade Thomas!" she screamed.

Nothing.

Serena surveyed the landscape. Just outside the door, there was a cloud. Maybe if she went to look for Zawade and came back really quickly, then that would be all right. After all, Moussa had said that she had physically retrieved him when she was a baby. It would be fine, she was sure.

She held her breath and took a step out of the train into the Great Unknown. Inside the tent, in the here and now, Serena's body collapsed onto the ground, next to the corpse of Zawade.

33

August 26th

A helicopter sped along the Atlantic Coast of Florida and touched down on a helipad at Ronnie Spade's sprawling mansion. Secret Service agents helped Queen Karen climb out of the chopper and then led her to Ronnie, who was waiting on the veranda.

"If it isn't my favorite fish!" he grinned, greeting Karen. "Welcome to Serenity-by-the-Sea." As he approached her, he noticed a foul odor, like something rotten, and he took several steps backward.

She picked up on his air of disgust. "I'm sorry about the smell, Ronnie. I have a few wounds that can't seem to heal."

He had planned to ask Karen to sit and have a Diet Coke with him, but now he reconsidered, repulsed by the idea of having her flesh touch his furniture. "Why don't we go for a walk around the property, Karen?"

He walked off, and she followed him.

When she caught up she asked, "Any word on Gia and the kid? Did your boys take them out?"

"They're not *my* boys, Karen!" he hissed, turning on her and lowering his voice conspiratorially. "Never say anything like that out loud! There could be listening devices anywhere! Bowden is desperate to nail me on something. He doesn't want to face a legitimate threat in the next election cycle."

"You're right," she agreed, bobbing her head. "There's no such thing as careful enough."

He nodded. "The truth is, Karen, things have been too quiet for my liking. I'm afraid that some of my allies may have been injured during that..." he turned his head side to side and then raised his voice, "HORRIBLE TERRORIST ATTACK." He darted his eyes back to her and then widened them, urging her on.

"Oh..." she replied, trying to follow his lead, "yes... can you IMAGINE what might lead someone to attack the heart of our military like that? It's awful. You know liberal terrorists are to blame since they hate this country and our servicemen and women."

He shook his head and leaned over, whispering in her ear, "You can't be stern and judgmental like that, Karen. You have to show these men love and respect... if a recording got leaked... it would... just be careful with your words."

She mouthed to him silently, "Gotcha."

They strolled along in silence until reaching a marble water fountain in the garden. Ronnie waved Karen over and spoke at a level that the water masked. "Do you have any suggestions on our next move?"

Karen's eyes danced like a devil's.

"Plenty," she replied. "But let's start by getting rid of Awa Diop."

* * *

AT LANGLEY MANOR, Harper and Queen Awa welcomed the Californian princes to their table.

"Have a seat, boys," Awa said. "Let's discuss what to do about that mother of yours."

Bryce scowled. "If Moussa had just left well enough alone, I would be in charge now, and we wouldn't be in this mess."

"It's *King* Moussa," Kyle snapped, "and he was trying to help."

Bryce glared at Harper. "Why are you here, Harper? Shouldn't you be down in D.C. covering the attack?"

"I'm on leave from work, Bryce. Don't you watch the news? I got kidnapped by a bunch of those psychos not that long ago."

Awa passed wine glasses around the table. "We're here as friends," she reminded everyone. "And we need to figure out what to do together. We each have a part to play."

The attack on the Pentagon had left Harper shaken. It wasn't just the fact that her niece was caught in the blast, and Harper didn't know if Serena was dead or alive. Watching the political situation devolve so quickly was highly disturbing. Harper had already been a target, and though it suited Ronnie Spade at the time to have her released, she knew she was still at the top of the militia's hit list. Having Awa take charge helped Harper feel less scared.

"Bryce," Awa continued, pouring him a glass of wine, "where do your people in California stand? Do they support your mother?"

"It's hard to say, Awa. I think that in many ways, they're still reeling from the shock of mourning her death and then watching her snap back to life. I know I am."

Awa took a few sips from her glass, thinking. "She drew her battle lines long ago, but now she's made them public. Declaring her intent to eliminate Gia was just the first step in a new plan. I'm certain of it. Aligning herself with Ronnie Spade gives her a national and international stage. And with Zale out of the picture, there's no doubt that she will move to become the leader of the Atargatic world. By attacking us in Senegal, she's already shown that she has no concern for the lives of our kind. She will destroy everyone who isn't loyal to her."

Bryce turned his gaze toward Kyle. The princes sighed, and Kyle lowered his head. "You're right," he said, finally. "I watched Mother gloat about destroying your colony and massacring your people. That's why I joined forces with Moussa. If we don't stop her, there's no telling what she will do."

Awa reached out and took Kyle's hand. "Darling, you did the right thing. You have a tender heart, and you are not at all like your mother."

Harper leaned in. "I have an idea."

Everyone looked in her direction, eager to hear her thoughts.

"Let's go to Washington," Harper said. "I'll interview you both in front of the ruins of the Pentagon. You should publicly denounce your mother for inciting violence and declare your intent to dethrone her. Try to peel Califonian support away from her. I'm assuming you'll have the backing of most of the Mermaid world, right?"

The princes turned to Awa for an answer on that. "At this point, only New Zealand is backing her. You'll have Senegalese support, of course. I know the Brazilians will side with you. Greece is a non-factor. I do think I can persuade the Japanese. Belize is always tough to nail down, but I really don't think they matter. And as for the Ice Folk..." Awa paused for a moment, thinking of the weapons and training exercises she had seen during her visit to the Arctic Circle.

She made direct eye contact with Bryce.

"The Ice Folk are ready for full-scale war."

34

Time Eternal

Serena was falling. She couldn't tell if she was falling up or falling down, because the sensation was strange, and she became disoriented as she passed through cloud after cloud. Had she been lucky enough to experience an actual childhood, perhaps her mother would have read her *Alice in Wonderland,* and she would have been reminded of Alice falling down the rabbit hole. But Serena had no such reference.

She finally landed, splashing into a pool of dark water. As her tail came in, she caught her breath, floating on the surface of the water. In the black sky, there were no stars, but she saw twenty moons, all a different color. The moons shone their iridescent sparkling light on the calm water. Serena realized she was in some kind of lake, but if there was a shore, she couldn't see it.

Behind her, there was a light splashing sound. She turned her head to investigate.

"Hey there, beautiful," said a woman to Serena. The lady was draped across a flamingo float, and she was sipping a cocktail out of a pineapple husk. "I've been hoping to run into you."

Serena studied the woman's face and squinted her eyes, trying to recall why she looked so familiar. "Do I know you?" she asked.

"Sure you do, kiddo. I'm a friend of your mom's. My name is Riley."

"I remember you now!" Serena replied, paddling over to Riley.

"I heard through the grapevine that you've been poking around in the afterlife."

"Where are we, Riley?"

"Ahhh," Riley sighed, "this place? It's where the bad folks go when they die."

Serena felt a shiver and her face must have showed her fright, because Riley started cackling.

"I'm joking! Kiddo, relax!"

Serena splashed Riley with her tail. "That's not funny!"

Riley laughed even harder. "Look, I'm not saying this is where the *best* people live out eternity... but I do think they keep the *really* bad ones somewhere else. Hmmm... I wonder... where do you think your mom will end up when she dies?"

The thought made goosebumps crawl down on Serena's arms, and she shook her head, trying to unspook herself. She decided that the best way to navigate this situation and keep her fear at bay was to focus on her mission.

"I'm searching for someone, Riley. Her name is Zawade Thomas. Have you seen her?"

Riley's green eyes twinkled with mischief. "Do you realize how big this place is?"

"No," Serena huffed, "I just got here."

"You're in luck," Riley said with a wink. "I think I know just who might be able to help us."

* * *

RILEY LED Serena into a forest made of tall mushrooms. The mush-trees glowed and pulsated—some seemed almost transparent. Serena reached out to touch one, but Riley smacked her hand away.

"Don't touch them," she warned. "They'll get you high as fuck."

There were whispers in the distance that wafted through the air, tickling Serena's ears. The voices repeated what Riley said in a mocking tone, "They'll get you high... they'll get you high!"

Serena grabbed Riley's hand out of fear. "Who's that?" she asked, trembling.

"Oh, they're just lost. Ignore them."

Riley marched on, twisting through the vibrant labyrinthian forest. "We're almost there. You're gonna love Su."

Serena was certain she saw people hiding behind the mushrooms, spying on them, and she felt herself automatically picking up her pace. This place creeped her out. She was very relieved when they reached the edge of the forest.

But then a heavy fog rolled in, enveloping them both. Serena held onto Riley even more tightly. The fog carried the same whispers Serena had heard in the forest, only there were many more voices. They walked for a long time, tormented by voices chittering in thousands of languages that Serena couldn't understand.

They reached an area where the fog lifted, and Serena could see the multi-colored light of the twenty moons in the sky again. A man was bent over a small pond, stirring the water with a jeweled spear. Serena only saw him from the back. He wore a silky robe that reflected the moonlight.

"Su, my man!" Riley said with a smile. "I brought you someone."

Su turned around. He was naked underneath his robes, and his body was covered with wet, blinking eyes.

Serena didn't mean to, but she screamed and stumbled backward.

Su's voice echoed around Serena, weaving itself to hold her like a snake. "Fear not, child. I am Susanoo, God of the Sea, God of the Storm. I am one thousand, and I am one."

Serena trembled uncontrollably. She wanted to run, but to where? She knew she would get lost in the fog or the forest of mushrooms and maybe never find Zawade or make her way home.

She couldn't bring herself to speak.

Thankfully, Riley spoke for her. "Serena is searching for some-one." Riley glanced down at Serena. "What's the name again?"

Serena's teeth chattered, and she tried to force words out, but no sound escaped. Riley crouched down and came near Serena.

"You're okay, kiddo. Tell me the name. Whisper it in my ear."

"Za...Zawade," Serena muttered. "Zawade Thomas."

Riley repeated it louder, "Zawade Thomas."

Su lifted his spear and sent a spark of electricity into the air. "Zawade Thomas, I command thy presence." He circled the spear round and round, and the lightning bolt twisted, thrashing out in all directions. It exploded in a bang and a flash of light, and a body fell from the sky, landing in the pond with a great splash.

It was Zawade.

She panicked, nearly drowning in the water. Serena rushed over to help her out. But when Zawade glimpsed Su's deformed body, she screamed just as Serena had.

"Help me, Riley!" Serena jumped in the pond and dragged Zawade to the edge. Riley helped to pull Zawade onto the ground.

"Leave me alone!" Zawade shouted. She struggled to get onto her feet and then pattered away into the fog.

Serena immediately chased after her. It was impossible to see in the haze, so Serena yelled Zawade's name over and over. Finally, she crashed into Zawade, who was sitting in a heap on the ground, sobbing.

"What is this place?" Zawade cried.

"I don't know," Serena admitted. "But we have to get you out of here. Your father wants you to come home."

"You can't take me back there," Zawade replied solemnly.

"I can, actually," Serena explained. "I've brought people back before."

"I know that," Zawade whispered. "They told me all about you."

"What? Who did?"

"I don't think I'm supposed to say."

Serena exhaled slowly and rubbed her arms to try to stop herself from trembling. She felt terrified and overwhelmed. She couldn't wait to figure out how to get out of here, get back to the land of the living, and make sure her mom was okay.

"You have to come with me," Serena insisted. "Your dad might do something bad to my mom if we don't go back."

"I can't."

"But you can. I'll take you. We can try to leave now."

"It's what *that monster* wants," Zawade whispered.

"Su?"

"I shouldn't say anymore. We should try to find the ladder."

"What are you talking about?"

"The ladder to the sky... the sisters are there."

"Serena?!" Riley's voice called out for her through the fog. "Where are you? Shout for me, and I'll find you."

Serena's pulse quickened. She suddenly had the impulse to run far away as fast as possible. For some reason, she didn't want Riley to find her.

"Let's go!" Serena pulled on Zawade's arm, forcing her up. "I don't want to go back to that pond. Let's look for the ladder."

35

Harper fidgeted with the bulletproof vest that fit her snugly under her blouse. In D.C.'s sticky morning air, it was uncomfortable and hot on her skin. She darted her eyes around the ruins of the Pentagon, surveying the landscape for phantom shooters.

The film crew was still setting up, and it was taking a long time. Too long.

"Hey," she called to the producer, "can we get a move on things? I really want to get this over with and go home."

Bryce and Kyle hung back, just off camera.

Kyle shook his head and exhaled. "This is disgusting. Look at this place... it's a giant graveyard. I shouldn't be surprised by anything our mother does, but this... it's worse than 9/11."

Bryce clenched his jaw and nodded in agreement. "It's sick. I wish I'd never helped her. She should be in jail... or fucking dead. If she were here right now, I'd kill her myself."

After a few more minutes, the broadcast began.

An OTN video drone flew over the bombed-out Pentagon,

streaming devastating footage to the viewers. Then the producers had a cross-fade transition to a closeup shot of Harper.

"Good morning, everyone. This is an OTN special report, live from the Pentagon. The extent of the damage and the loss of life here is absolutely devastating. A rescue mission is still very much under-way, as the desperate search for survivors trapped under the rubble continues. Early estimates predict that nearly twelve thousand lives were lost in this unprecedented attack. A white nationalist group called The Brotherhood has taken credit for the bombing. This is now the largest terrorist attack ever to have taken place on U.S. soil."

Harper took a deep breath to steady herself before continuing.

"The bombing took place mere days after former President Ronnie Spade and Queen Karen of California appeared on Klik Klak Live urging violence. Queen Karen Dean and Ronnie Spade asked their supporters to target my niece, Serena, and her mother, Gia Acquaviva. It is still unknown whether my... my ni—"

Harper's voice cracked, but she pressed on. "Whether my niece is alive or dead. There have been no reports from the remaining Pentagon officials regarding either Serena or her mother."

Harper glanced ever so slightly to her side and then said, "Joining me here today are Bryce and Kyle Dean, the sons and heirs to the throne of Queen Karen."

The camera cut to a wide shot of Harper and the Dean brothers.

"Bryce and Kyle, welcome to the show."

"Thanks for having us," Bryce replied.

"Bryce," Harper continued, "as you stand here, taking in all of this destruction, what goes through your mind?"

Bryce's complexion was pale, and his face appeared pinched. "This is horrifying. I almost can't fathom the enormity of what's happened, you know? I was recently released from custody regarding another attack that my mother was responsible for... in Senegal... nearly eight thousand merfolk. And thousands more were lost in the flood in Venice. My brother and I watch her racking up a death toll, and we feel—"

"It has to stop!" Kyle screamed, cutting in. "I don't even want to call this... this *monster* our mother. She has no regard for life. She doesn't care... she's totally devoid of normal brain function. If there is anything or anyone standing in the way of what she wants, she will destroy it."

Harper tilted her head. "And Kyle, can you shed some light on what Queen Karen meant when she said that Serena brought her back to life? Is that true?"

"Unfortunately," Kyle mumbled. "Our mother was very much dead. I watched her die myself."

"How is that possible? Can you explain that to our viewers?"

"Uh... sure. Strangely enough, Mother died trying to save Serena from being sacrificed by Queen Zale of Greece. Queen Zale killed Mother, using Ancient Magic. Then that caused Serena to... to be reborn... um... as an adult. And the new Serena... uh... she brought my mother back to life at her funeral."

Harper stared into the camera. While this was not news to her, she wondered what the OTN viewing public was making of this information.

"Wow. That's very complicated stuff, America."

Then she turned back to look at Bryce. "As usual, Gia Acquaviva is mixed up in all of this. When you see your mother going after Gia on social media, what do you think about that? Gia isn't an angel. She's got quite a death toll of her own."

"Look, one murder is too many murders, okay? I'm a zero murders kind of guy. But when you line up Gia against my mother... Gia's not out there committing genocide and ruining historic cities... and egging on domestic terrorists."

"So," Harper concluded, "you're saying that Gia is the lesser of two evils."

"Very much so."

"And Bryce, what is your plan moving forward? Do you think your mother is fit to rule the colony in California?"

"Absolutely not! My brother and I plan to challenge her claim to the throne. She needs to be removed from power. She should be rotting in jail."

Harper turned her attention back to the camera once more. "We'll be back with more after the break."

GIA HELD onto Serena's hand, stroking it. She had not left her daughter's side in days. General Thomas had set up a cot for her beside the bed where Serena laid, unconscious.

As for Zawade's corpse, the general had placed it in cold storage. He kept an eye on Gia from the other side of the tent.

An underling approached the general and whispered something in his ear. He rose to his feet and bolted off. A few moments later he returned with Queen Awa in tow.

Awa rushed over to Gia and threw her arms around her. "You're a cat, do you know that? How many of your nine lives have you used up by now? I'm so glad to see you. I truly am."

Gia was surprised by Awa's show of affection.

Awa glanced down at Serena and her expression soured. "Oh, Gia, I'm so sorry. Has Serena been like this since they rescued you? Is it a coma? What do the doctors say?"

Gia squeezed her eyes shut. "I do not know what has happened, Awa. Serena was fine, she was healthy... we survived the explosion. But..." Gia dropped the volume of her voice, so that the general couldn't hear her. "General Thomas forced Serena to reanimate his daughter who died in the bombings. Serena tried, but... then she fell and she has been like this for two days. The doctors said they don't know what has happened. They say that it looks to them like she is in a very deep sleep."

General Thomas approached the women. "We need to talk. Come with me."

"I do not want to leave my daughter," Gia replied.

"Let's go Acquaviva," he ordered. "Now!"

Gia blinked but did not move. "I am not scared of you, General. I have cut down men bigger than you. I buried them at the bottom of the sea."

"We're all aware of your *adventures*, Miss Acquaviva. I think you will want to hear what I have to say to both of you. It will benefit you greatly. If Serena wakes up, I'll send someone to notify us."

"*Bene*, take me where you wish, then." Gia's eyes lingered on Serena as the general led her out of the tent.

He showed Gia and Awa to a secure room and locked the door, approaching them. "What I am about to say to you can never leave this room. Is that understood?"

They both nodded their agreement.

"The current state of affairs is untenable. Ronnie Spade was always a liability to this country, but he has become an outright threat to democracy and the safety of the American people. I've spoken with President Bowden, and we're in agreement that Ronnie Spade must be *dealt with*. We would like your help with our problem."

His meaning was clear, and Awa and Gia's mouths dropped open in astonishment.

"Dealt with? You want us to *kill* Ronnie Spade for you?" Awa asked, almost laughing from the absurdity of it. "Don't you command the entire military apparatus of the United States? Why in the world would you need mermaids to do your dirty work?"

The general crossed his arms over his chest.

"Queen Awa, you rule a nation. You must understand the complexities of such power. Our military cannot be seen intervening in national affairs. It's what Ronnie wants. He's trying to kick off another civil war, and if I allow troops to get involved, then that's exactly what's going to happen."

Gia and Awa exchanged a worried glance.

The general continued. "On Labor Day Ronnie is set to have a large rally at his New York City hotel in Battery Park, right on the Hudson River. We have intel that Queen Karen and leadership from The Brotherhood will be present as well. We would like for you to assemble a small army and attack the rally. Target number one is Ronnie Spade. Gia, if you can give President Bowden what he wants, then he is prepared to wipe the slate clean for you. You won't face prosecution for your crimes."

Gia narrowed her eyes. "I would not dare to leave my daughter."

"We found Togashi this morning," the general replied. "He's fine... dehydrated, but fine. He can watch over Serena. Hopefully she will wake up soon and bring Zawade with her. I give you my word as a father that Serena will not be harmed."

Gia said nothing.

"Miss Acquaviva," the general finally said, "this is the best offer you're going to get. The President will deliver on his promise. I assure you that."

Awa reached out for Gia's hand and squeezed it. "Gia, this is not just about Ronnie Spade. We have to deal with Queen Karen. If we don't, then she will keep coming after you and Serena until she's won. You know that."

Gia's lips trembled.

Awa sucked her teeth and smiled slightly. "Come on, Gia! Moments ago you threatened a five-star general. What's so scary about a cheeseburger wearing a wig and an old, zombified queen?"

Gia whipped around to face General Thomas.

"Do you *swear* to me that Serena will remain safe and be here when I return."

"Of course," he replied.

Gia let out a huge sigh. "Let the president know that I will bring you Ronnie Spade's head on a plate."

36

August 27th

Secret Service agents oversaw the transfer of Awa and Gia to Harper's chauffeured Escalade. Once both women were safely ensconced inside, the guards left them in the hands of Harper's security detail.

Harper was waiting for them inside the car.

"Hi Gia," Harper said dryly, a smirk spreading across her face. "It's been a while."

"*Buonasera*," Gia replied, tossing her hair over her shoulder.

Harper's face softened, and she swallowed a lump in her throat. She inquired softly, "Is Serena... did Serena make it out...a–alive?"

"Why would *you* care, Harper?" Gia snapped.

Harper promptly rounded on her would-be sister-in-law. "She's my fucking *niece*, Gia! She's the only family I have left."

But Gia wasn't having it. "Serena is a bargaining chip for you, Harper. You never cared one bit about her. Otherwise you would not have been so willing to give her up."

Harper dug her nails into the leather of her seat. "That's not true at all."

"Ah, no?" Gia spat. "You traded her for help in killing your own parents. You appear on television under your studio lights with your big blonde hair and you present the picture of the perfect little person. But that is not *you*. You are as cold in your heart as I am, Harper. Maybe even more. I have known that since the first time we met in Venice. I have my reasons for the things I have done, but I would never hurt my own family!"

"Shut up, you stupid bitch!" Harper wailed. Tears flooded down her cheeks. "I lost my favorite person because of you. I wish Cameron had never met you, Gia. You're a fucking life ruiner, do you know that?"

"Ladies," Awa said, exhaling through her teeth. She placed one hand on Harper's knee and the other on Gia's. "I am not here to referee tonight. I understand that you each have justifiable, deep resentments, but you have to put all of that to the side. Especially right now, and hopefully for good. Whether you like it or not, you *are* family. Serena makes it so—she is the tie that binds you together, and she always will be. She's going to need both of you. So you have to stop reaching for one another's throats and learn to get along."

Harper wiped her eyes and resisted the urge to continue battling.

Gia sucked in her cheeks and turned her head toward the window.

It was going to be a long ride back to New York.

* * *

DURING THE LAST hour or so of the six-hour trip, Awa fell asleep. Therefore, Harper and Gia took turns shooting each other dirty looks. When the women finally rolled into the gates at Langley Manor, they were all exhausted.

Gia's stomach lurched when she saw the *porte-cochère*. Her thoughts instantly turned to Cameron and meeting his parents. Royce had been so charming, but Bronwyn... well, she and Harper had a lot in common as far as Gia was concerned. Harper displayed the same icy quality that Gia had found so off-putting in Bronwyn.

Cameron loved them so much, Gia thought. *He was not naïve. He saw them for who they were and loved them, regardless. Serena has that same goodness inside her... that innocence. I feel it.*

"Gia," Awa whispered, lifting Gia's haze of memories, "there is someone waiting inside to see you."

Gia hated surprises. "Who?" she asked, suspiciously.

Just then, the front door cracked open. Mariama emerged and walked up to the car door. Awa got out and hugged her wife, kissing her on the lips. Another figure loomed in the doorway.

Gia's heart flopped in her chest, and excitement fizzed through her veins.

It was Shadow.

She tried to steady herself and hold herself back from running to him and leaping into his arms. She scooted slowly out of the backseat and glided up the stairs, coming face to face with Shadow.

Gia began to ask him, "How did y—"

But she wasn't allowed to finish her question. He wrapped his arms around her, picking her up and kissing her deeply.

She relaxed into his embrace and let herself feel all the emotions bouncing around inside of her.

He pulled back slowly, gazing into her eyes, and said, "Don't scare me like that, love. At least now I know that I gotta keep both eyes on you. Trouble finds you, don't it?"

"I missed you, Shadow." Gia lifted her hand to his cheek, admiring him. "I missed you very much."

Harper passed by them on her way to the front door, narrowing her eyes in disgust. Frankly, she felt like shoving both of them down the stairs.

What a disrespectful bitch, Harper thought. *How dare she make out with some rando in front of me. Cameron would lose his shit about this. I will never understand why there is such a long line of men ready to fawn over Gia. She's a fucking psychopath.*

Oblivious to Harper, Shadow took Gia's hand, and they floated into the mansion in lockstep.

Mariama had asked the chef to prepare refreshments in the living room. Harper snatched a cup of coffee and plopped down on the sofa. Gia and Shadow curled into a loveseat.

"Fancy a biscuit and cuppa rosie?" Shadow asked.

Gia wrinkled her nose at him in confusion.

"Nevermind," he said, waving his hands. "Stay here." He stepped away to pour her a cup of tea. He placed a biscotti on a napkin and handed it to her.

"*Grazie mille*," Gia cooed.

As Gia sipped her tea, Awa brought in a tablet, propping it up on the coffee table. Awa logged onto a secure site and dialed Moussa from a videochat app.

"*Bonsoir*, everyone," he said, answering the call. "I am here with President João."

João waved hello.

Awa threaded her fingers together and pointed at the screen. "Gia and I have been given a mission, and we need your help. Moussa, João, I need you to gather your best fighters and come to New York."

"Fighters?" Moussa replied, perplexed. "For what, *Maman*?"

"Because," Awa replied, "we are going to kill Ronnie Spade."

37

August 28th

Shadow led Gia into the guest room at Langley Manor. With every step, she felt an eerie presence—maybe it was Cameron's ghost hovering nearby. Or maybe it was simply his memory haunting her. The room was the same one where she'd slept with Cameron, and the bed was the one they'd made love in.

Her memories flashed in her mind: him touching her belly, talking about their baby, and fantasizing about domesticating Gia.

At the time, she had felt suffocated by Cameron's desires and the very idea of such a long-term commitment, but now she found herself regretting the fact that they never even had the chance to explore parenthood together. She sat on the edge of the bed and ran her hands across the duvet.

Shadow approached her, reaching down and lifting her chin. She gazed up at him.

"Gia, you been through a lot." He caressed her cheek. "Too much for one person. Come here."

He slid his arms around her shoulders and pulled her closer. She rested her head on him, and he stroked her hair.

"You deserve someone to look after you," he said.

Do I? Gia wondered. *I am not sure I deserve much of anything after all I have done.*

She sighed, troubled by her thoughts and self-reflection.

"Shhh," Shadow whispered. "You got me now, and everything's gonna be all right, love."

He arched her head back and held it in his palm. With the other hand, he brushed her hair away and ran his fingers down her neck. She felt a tickle as his hand passed over her shoulder, and she smiled.

"You like that?" he asked, his voice gruff.

"Mmhmm," she purred.

He grinned. "Oh, I been waitin' a long time for this." He pressed her down onto the bed and kissed her behind her ear. "Let's get you outta these clothes."

He lifted her, removing her shirt. He glanced at her bra—and at her plump breasts—and sighed.

"Fuckin' hell. You're more beautiful than I imagined. I wanted to sneak a peek when we were hidin' out together in France, but I'm too much of a gent, ya see."

He slid off her pants, making sure to be careful of her leg, which had just barely healed from the hairline fracture. He lightly kissed her shin.

He took off his shirt, and Gia drank him in, exploring his muscles with her hands. He scooped her up and placed her in the middle of the bed, straddling her. She wrapped her legs around his waist, and he kissed her, sliding his tongue across hers.

They rocked back and forth together for quite some time until he reached into his pocket and pulled out a condom. He was just about to rip it from the corner when she shook her head and cupped her hand over his.

"Leave it," Gia insisted.

"But I don't wanna get you preg—"

"Shh," she whispered, putting her finger on his lips. "I want all of you."

He tossed the condom on the floor and stripped off his pants.

His cock was thick and hard. Gia stroked it several times before Shadow spread her legs and pressed inside her.

Gia exhaled sharply and then bit down on his shoulder.

"Yes," he groaned, "Bite me harder."

She sunk her teeth deeper into his muscle and traced her hands down his hips and back, around him. She slid her hands down to his ass, bringing him closer to her, making sure every inch of him was buried deep inside her.

After a while, she brought her mouth close to his ear and said, "I want to go on top."

Without removing himself, he flipped her over, so that he was lying down, and he propped his head on the headboard. She curled her legs around him and pressed her hips into him, so that she could feel both his cock inside her and the friction from rubbing her clit on his pelvis.

"Jaysus," he cried.

He took her breasts in one hand, smashing them together. He smacked her ass with the other hand, and she yelped in pleasure.

"Again," she commanded.

He sucked on her nipple and shook his head no.

"Please," she begged. "I am so close."

He opened his mouth and let his tongue drag across both nipples. "I said no."

Gia whimpered, and he gathered up all her hair and yanked it slowly back.

There was a glint in his eye. "You'll come when I say so."

He moved his hips back and forth, arching her body as he went. Gia breathed harder and harder. He licked her breasts and bit her nipple softly. Finally, he pulled her head close to him and said, "Open your eyes."

She opened them.

"Cum for me, Gia."

Her eyelashes fluttered as he spanked her hard several more times. She felt her orgasm flowing through her, radiating from between her legs. Everything tingled, even her lips.

"That's right," he whispered. "Come on my cock."

And she did.

When she finished, she fell limp, collapsing on his chest.

"You're sure it's fine for me to cum inside you?" he asked.

"I want you to," she insisted.

He turned her over again, sliding gently in and out of her, taking his cock out and then repositioning it again and again, massaging the tip by dipping it into her.

"Give me everything," she pleaded.

And he did.

He laid down on top of her until his cock went soft inside her.

Shadow rolled beside her and kissed her neck. Then he asked, "You all right?"

"After all that?" she giggled. "I feel quite revived. We might have to do it again."

He smiled, shaking his head. "Give a geezer a few minutes to come back full speed."

She kissed his chest and laid her head down over his heart. She could hear it beating fast.

"I made love to Cameron in this bed," she whispered, sighing. As soon as she'd said it, she wished she hadn't.

But Shadow didn't mind. He was well aware of her past and didn't resent her for it. After all, he had a sordid past, too,

In reality, he knew that Cameron was long gone, Florent, too, and even Riley. Gia was his now.

"Don't worry about all that," he replied. "What's in the past stays there. It's you and me from now on, love."

38

Time Eternal

S erena and Zawade raced through the fog, trying to find their way out of this realm and escape to the sky via the ladder to the moons.

They reached the edge of the fog and found themselves facing the mushroom forest. The mush-trees were shaking and bobbing, glowing even brighter than they had when Riley had taken her through the forest moments before. Upon closer inspection of the mushrooms' pillowy skin, Serena realized that people were trapped inside the stems. They appeared to be sleeping—or they were dead. She couldn't be sure.

Zawade tugged on Serena's arm. "Let's go this way!" Zawade skirted the edge of the forest until they reached a tunnel made of glass.

Zawade ducked inside, and Serena followed.

Inside the tunnel, images from the World of the Living appeared. Serena saw her mother at various times throughout her life. The images cycled through, out of order. Sometimes Gia was very young, and at other times, older. Serena watched the murders, too. She saw her mother strike down people, slitting their throats and hiding their bodies. Serena squeezed her eyes shut, trying to block out the truth about her mother, and she kept running.

They emerged on the other side of the tunnel at a door.

Zawade knocked three times and then opened it.

There, floating in space and extending high into the sky, was a ladder.

Serena jumped onto it and it swung far to the right. It took all of her strength to hold on.

She wasn't sure where she might land should she fall off the ladder. And she certainly didn't want to find out.

* * *

THE LANDS beyond the sky were warmer and brighter than the crisp, moonlit darkness of the underworld. Less eerie, too.

Here, Serena found things that were familiar, like clouds and flowers. In the distance, there was a cottage surrounded by a splendid garden. A woman snipped a rose off a tall shrub, placing it in a basket.

"That's Tsukuyomi," Zawade explained. "Goddess of the Sun."

They approached the goddess slowly.

"Pardon me," Serena said, "Zawade insisted that we seek you out."

Tsukuyomi cut another rose from the bush and extended it toward Serena. "A gift for an extraordinary child."

Serena took it and bowed her head. "Thank you."

"How is the beast?" Tsukuyomi inquired.

Zawade responded, "He's up to the same tricks you described."

"Interfering in human affairs?"

Zawade nodded.

"One would think that with thousands of eyes, he might be able to see the truth, yet he continues on, clinging to his dreams of destruction."

Tsukuyomi sighed, turning toward the cottage. Zawade followed, so Serena went as well. Tsukuyomi knocked three times before entering.

Inside, there was another woman, standing in the kitchen kneading dough. "The child arrived on time," she said, looking up at Serena.

"Indeed," Tsukuyomi replied to her sister goddess. She then folded herself into an armchair near the hearth.

Tsukuyomi's sister eyed Serena, inspecting her from head to toe. Although to Serena, it felt like the woman was looking through her. "I suppose you are very confused, Serena."

Serena frowned, unsure of what to say. She'd never met a goddess, let alone two. Her life was confusing and strange, so this latest adventure was no different. She desperately did long for someone—hopefully this goddess—to explain everything to her in a way that made sense. And after that, she wanted to go home and take Zawade with her.

"We hear that you have been raising the dead," the woman said, lifting an eyebrow. "We wish you would not."

Serena's skin went all prickly. "I didn't know that."

"With every soul you return to the land of the living, our brother's power grows stronger."

"Your brother... he's that monster I met?"

"The Great Susanoo," Tsukuyomi cackled.

"And who are you?" Serena asked humbly.

"I am Ameratsu, Ruler of the Moon. You set me free."

"I did?"

Ameratsu nodded. "With the help of my sister and your grand-mother, of course."

"I'm sorry. I really don't understand what you mean."

"Why would you?" Ameratsu shrugged.

Tsukuyomi rose and placed her hand on Serena's shoulder. "You will come to understand in time."

"I really need to go home," Serena explained. "And I have to take Zawade with me."

"We cannot stop you," Ameratsu admitted.

Tsukuyomi sighed. "The choices you make on your journey must be your own. Whatever you decide, know that you have the capacity to cause great suffering or great joy. It may be difficult to discern the difference at times."

Ameratsu led Serena and Zawade to the front door. She knocked once and turned the knob.

It opened into a train car.

Serena recognized it as the train between this universe and her own.

"Come on, Zawade, let's go."

Zawade backed up. "I'm not going back."

"You have to," Serena pleaded. "If you don't, something bad might happen to my mother."

"If I go with you, other terrible things might happen."

Serena took a deep breath and steeled herself. Then, she grabbed Zawade and jumped onto the train.

39

September 3rd

On the Hudson River, at a defunct fishing warehouse thirty minutes south of Langley Manor, Queen Awa, Gia, and Shadow hid in the darkness.

Under the cover of nightfall, a lazy barge drifted in, anchoring near a pier outside the warehouse. After a moment or two, Moussa and President João stepped off the boat, making their way into the warehouse with haste.

"*Maman*?" Moussa called out.

"Over here, Son," Awa replied, pulling a string to turn on a soft yellow light.

"Who is this?" João asked, pointing at Shadow.

"I'm Shadow London," he replied, extending his hand to the Brazilian president.

João glanced over at Awa, "But *who* is he?"

"Relax, João," Awa replied. "He's with us."

"Is he Senegalese? I have not seen him around in Rio."

"I'm from London," Shadow responded. "From under London."

"What are you talking about?" João snapped. "Queen Awa, you told us to be discreet, and yet, here is a stranger... some human."

"I ain't human," Shadow growled. "You Atargatic merms think you're the only ones... but you don't know that there's a whole network of brackish colonies you've never even heard of."

"It's true, João," Awa explained. "Shadow has been working with Gia for some time now. He was present at the Salt Cathedral when Karen and Zale fought."

João was still staring at Shadow, unconvinced.

Awa laughed. "I've seen his tail myself."

"Apologies," João conceded. "I suppose I am a bit on edge."

"Understandable," Shadow replied. "Ain't every day that you get a mission to kill an American president."

João sighed. "Precisely, sir."

"And the soldiers?" Awa asked.

Moussa nodded. "They're here. In the belly of the barge. Around two hundred between the Senegalese and the Brazilians."

"Good," Awa whispered to herself. "The Ice Folk will be here tomorrow. They realize this is a human conflict, but they agree that it's as good of a time as any to try to take out Karen. Should we have our troops unload and sleep here in the warehouse?"

"No, no," Moussa replied. "They have sleeping bags. They're fine on the ship."

Awa reached out for her son's hand. "Such a good king you are. I am so proud of you."

He smiled and said, "You taught me everything, *Maman*."

"Come and gather around me." Awa motioned everyone toward her. "Let's review the maps that General Thomas gave us."

Gia took a deep breath and stepped forward.

40

September 3rd

A thousand thoughts and worries swam in Gia's head.

What if everything goes wrong? What if I am killed in the attack, and Serena is left without parents like I was? What if we lose?

Shadow approached her, reaching out for her with both hands. He tapped gently on her temple. "What's goin' on in that loaf of bread?"

"Nothing, *amore*," she replied.

"Hmm... I doubt that very much. Here's what I think... I think you're used to planning every detail of your kills. Spending months watching them, learning everything about them." He pulled her close to him and whispered in her ear. "Fantasizing about the moment when they'd stop breathing."

He was right. Gia bit her lip, feeling electricity at his words.

"And now," he continued, "nothing's on your terms. You're more or less a hired gun."

She frowned.

He slid his hand down to her ass and squeezed it. "Which makes you just the same as me, don't it?"

He kissed her deeply.

"I am scared, *amore,*" she admitted.

"Don't be," he insisted. "I will be with you every step of the way. Ain't nothing bad gonna happen to my bird."

She rested her head on his shoulder.

"One more thing," he whispered. "I don't want you calling me *amore.* It's what you called Florent." He squinted at her, studying her face. "And probably every other sad sack you ever got your hands on. So, we're gonna start fresh, you and me. Call me... call me the love of your life."

"How presumptuous!"

"Nothing presumptuous about it. I'm not letting you get away from me, Gia Acquaviva. I *am* the love of your life. You'll see."

She pouted and held her gaze on him for a long time.

Finally he said, "I set up a little bed for us in a fishing boat outside. Come with me."

He led her out to the small marina outside the warehouse. They climbed into the old wooden boat, and he laid down on the floor, lifting a blanket. She cuddled up to him.

They stared up at the night sky. Long, thin clouds wafted through the air, caressing the moon. It was a first quarter moon, and it shone in the sky like half a silver coin.

"I spoke to *La Nonna* this morning," Shadow said.

"Did you?"

"Unfortunately, it's not good news."

Gia sat straight up. "What is it?"

"She's having trouble getting back any of your assets."

"*Any* of them?"

"The clubs... the properties..."

"And my bank accounts?" Gia asked fearfully, not really wanting to hear his answer.

He grimaced. "Still frozen."

"*Merda*! Why are you only telling me this now? I want to call her!"

"Shhh!" Shadow glanced around and dropped his volume. "Be careful, Gia. We have to stay quiet."

She crossed her arms in front of her chest. "So then I have nothing?"

"Not *nothing.*"

"What then?"

He sighed. "*La Nonna* said that Monaco might be willing to play ball."

She glared at him.

"Don't look at me like that, little miss," he teased. "Do you expect there to be no consequences for all those murders? Come on now. You might not have your fortune, but you got your freedom. That's worth a lot more, surely?"

"True," she huffed. "Then... the casino in Monte Carlo... are they willing to let me have it?"

"Not exactly."

"Ah, Shadow! Stop this and just tell me plainly what to expect."

"They might be willing to give you back your yacht... if you relinquish control of the casino."

"My yacht?!"

Shadow put his finger to his lips, warning her once again to be quiet.

She lowered her voice. "And how do they expect me to survive with no money? How am I to service the boat, to staff it, to maintain it?"

"I'm pretty handy."

"This is not a joke, Shadow."

"Gia, love, I told you this before. You're the biggest baddie there is. You'll figure it out. *We'll* figure it out. Okay?"

She plunked herself on the bottom of the boat beside him and turned onto her stomach.

I refuse to be poor, Gia thought.

"You know," he said, his voice sounding a little sparkly. "I got some money of my own."

"I do not want your money. I want *my* money." Her thoughts

drifted to Florent, and she shivered, remembering how it felt to be at his mercy.

"I understand." He stroked her hair and let his fingertips glide across her scalp. Gia found it deeply relaxing. "Let's take things one step at a time."

"Shadow?"

"Yes?"

"Make love to me."

"That's a very good first step," he replied, tugging her shirt down to kiss her shoulder.

41

September 4th

Skirlor and the Ice Folk appeared before dawn, five hundred tails thrashing underwater. Several naval airships had carried them to a secret location in the Atlantic. The planes hovered low enough over the ocean for the Ice Folk to dive out into the open water. After two days of swimming, they had finally arrived at the fishing warehouse to meet Gia and the others.

Skirlor greeted Queen Awa and then escorted her underwater to see the troops. She was surprised to see that while they carried ice spears, there was no sign of the larger scale weapons she'd seen during her visit to the Arctic Circle. Once they were back in the warehouse, Awa pulled him off to the side for a private word.

"Pardon me for saying so, Skirlor," Awa said, "but you seem under armed."

Skirlor tutted. "No, we have all the power you need, I assure you."

"If you say so."

João waved them over. "We need to review the plans again," he insisted.

"Let's wait for Bryce and Kyle to get here," Moussa replied. "They're coming with twenty Californians."

"Is that *all*?" Awa balked.

"*Maman*," Moussa fussed, "they're doing the best they can. At the moment, the colony is still ruled by Queen Karen. Her subjects have proven to be annoyingly loyal."

* * *

AWA POINTED to a map of Manhattan. "That's Battery Park. And there, that's Ronnie's hotel, the Imperial Spade. You see, it backs up to the park and there's a pier right next to the hotel. Ronnie is using the hotel's event venue on the river as a stage, and then the rally will overflow into Battery Park."

"How many people are they expecting?" Bryce asked.

Awa frowned. "Every hotel in Lower Manhattan is booked solid. There could easily be ten thousand or more people there."

"Ten thousand!?" Bryce balked. "Jesus, we're what... less than eight hundred?"

Awa patted him on the back. "Don't focus on that, Bryce. Now," she said, turning her head, "Skirlor, you will lead the first wave. Break up into three units." She pointed to the map in different locations. "Approach from here, here, and here."

He nodded his head once in acknowledgment.

"I want maximum confusion," Awa explained. "We should try to minimize casualties. Apparently there is supposed to be a large group of Brotherhood members guarding Ronnie Spade. We should take them out. I expect the crowd to be heavily armed."

She glanced around the room at her friend's faces. They looked worried.

"Gia and Shadow, you should slip in here." She had marked in red a spot on the map near the hotel. "That is a drainage pipe right next to the stage. It should give you pretty direct access. Kyle, Bryce... take your twenty Californians and guard Gia and Shadow. It's essential that Gia gets to Ronnie Spade."

"Okay," Kyle replied. "Roger that."

Moussa's stomach dropped at the thought of losing Kyle the way he'd lost Oumar.

"Are you sure, *Maman*?" Moussa asked. "Wouldn't it be better for me to go with some of our fighters?"

"You, King Moussa," she said, "along with President João and the joint troops... will round out the back. I want you to press in from the other side and crush Ronnie Spade's security from behind."

* * *

GIA STARED out at the river as the sun set across the Hudson. Her mind drifted back to the Thanksgiving she'd spent at Langley Manor with Cameron. Her thoughts were pulled to a specific memory: whipping through the country roads in the little sports car that Cameron had driven.

In Washington, Serena said that Cameron forgave me, Gia thought. *What would have happened if he had lived? Would I have killed him like all the others?*

She searched herself, trying to take stock of her life. *What do I want from now on? If the general does wipe the slate clean for me, how long will it be before I crave blood again? Will I really be able to focus on motherhood? How does one even raise a child who is already grown? And Shadow... do I feel as strongly about him as he does about me? He seems so sure of what he wants. How can I possibly start over at this point in my life?*

"Earth to Gia," Shadow whispered, approaching her.

"Hmm?" she murmured, turning to face him.

"I've been calling out to you for a bit. You're lost in your thoughts."

She shook her head, as if trying to clear cobwebs.

"Are you worried about tomorrow, Gia?"

"Of course. If something happens to me... or... if I cannot do what has been asked of me, then... I fear what might happen to Serena."

Shadow took her hand and kissed it. "We will spill blood together, love. I will make certain you get to that day-glow demon and slaughter him."

"Why?" Gia's chest suddenly felt heavy. "Why are you here helping me?"

"Ouch," he replied, sucking air through his teeth. "Hurts you even gotta ask me that." He grabbed her head with both hands and kissed her on the forehead. "Coz I'm in love with you, you stubborn cow."

"It feels strange, Shadow."

"What does? Your heart?"

"*I* feel strange."

He chuckled. "That's 'cause you never had a man as bad as you by your side. Everything in my black, rotten little heart loves everything in yours. We're the same, you and me."

"Is that so?"

"I am many things, Gia, but I ain't a liar."

What is it that is holding me back? Gia wondered. *He must be a killer... otherwise he would not be a hard man at all. But he is not like Riley. She was passionate... but insecure. Shadow is so sure of himself, so steady, solid.*

Gia heard footsteps shuffling behind her.

It was Queen Awa.

"Pardon me," Awa said. "I don't mean to interrupt you, but it's time for us to set sail."

Gia's heart lurched. She glanced over at Shadow.

He winked at her and smiled.

"We got this," he whispered.

42

Labor Day

Ronnie Spade peered out of the two-story windows in his gold-plated suite on the top floor of his hotel. He admired the amassing crowd below. The sun was fat and juicy. There wasn't a cloud in the sky. It was going to be a perfect day—he just knew it.

He puckered his lips around a straw and sucked in several large gulps of Diet Coke before opening his mouth as wide as it could go, letting out an earth-shaking belch.

"Ah, that's better," he mumbled to himself, patting his tummy.

He opened his bedroom door and yelled past the Secret Service agents posted outside of it. "Karen! Get in here!"

Queen Karen hobbled across the massive suite.

"Do you need me, Mr. President?" she asked.

"I'm in a good mood today, Karen." He sipped from his can of soda and then smacked his lips. "A very generous mood. In fact, I'm going to give you a gift."

"Sir," she replied, grinning, "simply being here with you is a gift, in and of itself."

He puffed his bloated lips into a pout. "No one likes an ass-kisser, Karen."

She almost chuckled. Of course he liked ass-kissers. The man was, indeed, surrounded by them at every level. Ronnie Spade was nothing if not delusional, and she idolized him for it. After all, he'd fashioned himself into the most famous person alive. Karen knew there was much she could learn from him.

"My gift, Karen, is that I am going to let you give a little speech after I finish talking. Normally I don't do that. Usually after my speech, a band plays, or dancers perform... something like that. But today, I want to let my supporters know that you have my stamp of approval. You've got a lot of potential, and I've been kicking around a few ideas about how best to use your talents. I'm thinking that after my re-election, we should run you for California governor. You've got money, and you've got years and years of leadership experience. In fact, I think that you could bring a very interesting perspective to conservative politics. We can really work that 'back from the dead' angle for the Jesus freaks. And, of course, all the save-the-whales nuttos will love your... uh... your *fish ancestry*."

"I'm flattered, sir."

She was more than flattered; Karen was elated. Ronnie Spade dangled before her exactly the kind of power she had always dreamed about but never imagined she could actually achieve. She relished in the thought of expanding her influence. There was something so small-minded about mermaids like Queen Zale, who focused all their attention on underwater affairs. Karen knew that if she was going to make an impact and leave a real legacy, she would have to do so on solid ground.

Ronnie shoved a few fast food napkins at her—they were covered in the ink from a black Sharpie. "Here, I made some notes for you. Study these talking points, and let's run some lines later."

He turned heel, and started off in the direction of his bedroom, but circled back for a final word.

"Oh, Karen... let's not mention the Pentagon stuff, okay? It's all kind of hairy at the moment with that. My lawyers are trying to swat away a possible investigation."

* * *

A RETIRED COUPLE FROM OGLETHORPE, Georgia, posed for a photo in Battery Park, donning their red Ronnie Spade baseball caps. A young man from New Jersey tried to pose them in such a way as to include the Statue of Liberty in the image.

"Move to the left a little," the young man shouted to the couple.

They scooted, but he wasn't happy with the photo he snapped on the old man's iPhone. He walked over and handed the phone back to them.

"Sorry," he said. "I tried to get a clean shot of Lady Liberty, but that ugly barge is blocking the view."

The couple turned around to see a hulking blue barge stacked sky-high with shipping containers.

"Dammit!" the old woman cursed at the phone as she swiped through the ruined photos. "Thanks anyway, Son."

They all walked away.

But the barge remained, slowly drifting in the Hudson River between Lower Manhattan and Ellis Island.

It had been somewhere just above the Bronx that the mermaid army had snuck off of the barge and slipped into their positions underwater. The barge itself was nothing more than a distraction— the tip of the iceberg, so to speak.

Gia and Shadow separated themselves from the bigger group, taking with them Bryce and Kyle and the twenty Californians. They paddled to the base of the Hudson, where a storm drain connected the river to a system of tunnels below Manhattan. They removed the heavy metal grate and disappeared, one by one, into the darkness.

* * *

ROCK MUSIC BLARED through the speakers outside the Imperial Spade and echoed through Battery Park. The LED screens throughout the area lit up, and motion graphics sprang to life. They read, "IT'S SHOWTIME, FOLKS!"

There were thousands upon thousands of rabid fans clamoring to get closer to the stage. NYPD, event staff, and members of The Brotherhood worked together to control the crowd.

A cheer broke out and the crowd chanted, "RONNIE! RONNIE! RONNIE!"

Ronnie Spade stepped onto the stage brandishing a t-shirt gun like Rambo, and he fired at the crowd indiscriminately, launching his signature merch in every direction.

He strolled to his podium, taking the time to soak in every ounce of obsessive love that was emanating from his supporters.

He leaned his head down and whispered into the mic. "Did I hear you call my name?"

The revelers lost it. They howled, and some even shed actual tears. It was like he was a Beatle—albeit a puffed-up, spray-tanned, and sweating Beatle.

Ronnie spread his lips into what he thought looked like a genuine smile. "Hello all you beautiful people! Welcome to my city... to New York City! Now, the *other* New Yorkers hate it when I call it *my* city. But who cares about those losers? We're the winners! And you know what? We're going to win big time, and we're going to get back to the White House, and we're going to set this country straight! What do you say about that?"

The crowd screeched and hooted, delighted by every word he spoke.

"I have a special guest joining me today. You've probably seen her on that whickaty whackady Klik Klakky app with me. Everyone... give a round of applause for Queen Karen Dean of California!"

Karen floated onto the stage, beaming and waving to the crowd.

Ronnie craned his head around and shooed Karen away. "Now, now, Karen... it's not your turn yet. Go stand at the back of the stage." Then he turned his attention back to the audience. "We're going to give Old Karen a few moments to talk, but not until I'm finished. Because I need you, and you need me, isn't that right?"

Suddenly, something very shiny flashed in Ronnie's eyes, blinding him for a moment. He blinked several times and tried to regain his vision.

At the edge of the water, he caught sight of something he found really strange. There was a figure in the distance with translucent skin, holding...

"What is that?" Ronnie whispered to himself. "Is that... a *battle ax*?"

Before he could say or see anything more, the Secret Service had surrounded him.

On the bank of the river, a wave of Ice Folk folded into the crowd at the rally.

The old woman from Georgia screamed at the top of her lungs when she crossed paths with Skirlor. He swung an ice hammer at her head gently enough to knock her out, but not to kill her. The Brotherhood rushed forward into the crowd, clearly hell bent on attacking the Ice Folk. At that same moment, the second wave of the Ice Folk struck, coming from a different direction.

The NYPD captain on site shouted into a loudspeaker, "STAND BACK OR WE'LL SHOOT!"

The Ice Folk launched a hailstorm of spears in the direction of the cops. The loudspeaker fell to the ground with a hissing thud after the captain was impaled through the head. Shots rang out as the police returned fire.

At the far end of Battery Park, the third wave of Skirlor's troops marched in. A sea witch was in their midst, and she flailed her arms around wildly, casting spells that tied up groups of people with magical ropes made of ice.

The scene was so chaotic that no one even noticed when a manhole near the stage lifted. Shadow poked his head out enough to survey the area. He sent the Calfornians out first, toward the stage, and hung back with Gia.

The Secret Service had initiated their standard security protocol and were attempting to move Ronnie Spade into a panic room in the hotel's basement, but they were cut off by the fighters from California.

A gunshot fired, then another and another.

Ronnie's eyes spun in their sockets. He didn't know where to look. "Get me inside!" he screeched, desperate to save his own skin above all else.

One of the agents near him was struck with an ice sword and collapsed.

Queen Karen spotted Ronnie in distress and began chanting, casting a spell of her own. Within a minute, a small tornado of water whipped its way from the river to the stage, taking out a line of fighters.

"Mother!" Bryce screamed, running up to Queen Karen from behind. "Stop that!"

She tried to turn around to face her son, but was tackled by a Brazilian soldier. Moussa, Awa, and João had just arrived with their two hundred fighters thrashing about.

"Let her go! I'll deal with her!" Bryce yelled. He sprinted toward her, but he never made it. He was shot through the stomach by a Brotherhood leader's AR-15.

"Bryce!" Queen Karen yelped, forgetting about her spell. "Oh, Jesus... Bryce!" She broke loose and scrambled over to him. By the time she got to him, he was coughing up blood.

Bryce raised his bloody hand and pointed a shaky finger at his mother. "You... did... this."

She backed away from him. "No... no."

Bryce's whole body trembled. Queen Karen saw Kyle in the distance, and she took off running, prioritizing self-preservation— plus, she couldn't bear seeing Kyle watch his brother die. Karen spotted the open manhole, and she shimmied down the ladder, escaping.

In the mayhem, the tides seemed to be turning. The humans were fighting back, gaining ground. There were simply not enough merfolk. Skirlor jittered in a high-pitched howl and signaled for his troops to fall back.

The Senegalese and Brazilians were going head to head with the Brotherhood—and losing.

Shadow and Gia hid behind a curtain, watching everything unfold and waiting for the moment to strike out toward Ronnie Spade.

Gia kept her eyes trained on Ronnie. The few Secret Service agents still left guarding the ex-president began to walk him slowly into the building.

"Shadow, look," Gia whispered, pulling his arm. " Ronnie Spade is getting away. We have to go now!"

Shadow wrapped his arm around Gia's waist. "No! Wait! This isn't the right moment."

"It is the *only* moment!" Gia cried. "Let me go after him!"

"Not a chance in hell I'm letting you go."

Shadow turned his head to look out at the crowd. The numbers of merfolk were dwindling rapidly. He watched Awa strangle a member of the Brotherhood and wrangle away his weapon. She herded Moussa, Kyle, and the remaining Senegalese and Brazilian troops to the side of the stage.

"Things don't look good, Gia. I think we—"

Before Shadow could even finish what he was saying, his breath froze into tiny, icy particles. The intense drop in air pressure and temperature was so severe that he completely lost his train of thought.

A thunderous shriek exploded into the air, capturing everyone's attention.

"What the hell is going on?" Gia asked Shadow, her body shivering from the cold.

The skies turned grey, and the Hudson River churned violently. A tidal wave splashed ashore, its water freezing as it traveled across the ground. Skirlor appeared again, and he faced the river, shouting orders in his strange native language. Thousands of Ice Folk materialized, stepping out of the frozen tidal wave. One sea witch cast a spell to call forth a kraken. The Ice Folk fanned out in tight formations, slaughtering every human in sight.

"We have to leave!" Shadow yelled, pushing Gia. "Let's get out of here!"

Gia ignored him and bolted from the curtain toward the hotel door she'd seen Ronnie go through. Shadow grabbed onto her. "Forget about Ronnie Spade!"

"Shadow," she pleaded, "please, help me. I have to try to get to him, for Serena's sake."

Shadow's eyes darted around the park, searching for backup. He spotted Awa. He knew it would only be a matter of time before the NYPD called in every available cop to fight off the latest wave of Ice Folk.

Their time was running out. But he knew Gia was right.

They had to find Ronnie.

43

Labor Day

Ronnie Spade hid in the panic room that was housed at the Imperial Spade, guarded by his five remaining Secret Service agents.

"What's the plan guys?" he asked, his veneers chattering in fear. "We can hide in here for a while, but how are you planning to get me out? I need to talk to the media. I have to address this massacre. It can't look like I'm some kind of coward. That won't play well with my followers."

CLANG!

Something hard landed on the outside of the metal door of the panic room. The concrete floor vibrated below their feet.

CLANG!

"Do something!" Ronnie screamed.

The agents removed their guns from their holsters.

CLANG!

Another thud landed against the door, but this time, it made a huge dent and then—

PLINK! PLINK! PLINK! PLINK!

The door cracked into a million pieces, dissolving into small bits of metal. They crashed down and spread into the room like sand across the floor.

Ronnie gasped and screamed, "What the fuck?!"

Nothing remained of the door, and Skirlor stepped through its empty frame.

Ronnie hid behind his Secret Service agents, taking cover with his human shields. The men fired their weapons, but nothing happened when they pulled the triggers. Their guns were completely frozen.

Awa slipped into the room, and Shadow and Gia followed in her wake.

Immediately the Secret Service agents launched into hand-to-hand combat, but Skirlor made easy work of them. He chanted a spell that tied the agents together with an ice rope. They could still scream, of course—not that it helped them.

Ronnie tried to run for the door but his path was blocked by Shadow. Awa sprinted behind Ronnie and immobilized him, grabbing both his arms and twisting them behind his back.

"Remember me?" Awa inquired to his left ear, a giant smile on her face.

He nodded, his eyes wide with fear. "You're the Queen of Senegal."

"Mmm, what a good memory you have." Awa turned her gaze to Gia. "Come, do it now."

"Do *what*!?" he cried.

Gia took careful steps in Ronnie's direction. The muscles in her right arm twitched as the gill under her skin ruffled, unfurling itself.

"No, no... listen... Gia... I can give you anything you want. I'm the President of the United States of America for God's sake. Anything you want, just name it."

Gia ran her fingers along the scalloped edges of her gill. It was so sharp that she inadvertently pricked herself. A drop of blood splashed on the concrete—it was something Ronnie noticed, and he let out a squeal.

Her eyes were trained on Ronnie's and her heart beat wildly in her chest as anticipation bubbled inside of her. An erogenous jolt of energy pulsed through her body as she took her final step.

Fascinating, she thought. *I still love killing, even if I am a hired woman, as Shadow said.*

Gia lifted her right arm in the air and hovered it there for a moment. She caught a glimpse of Shadow lurking in the corner of the room. She focused her eyes on him and suddenly felt a bit self-conscious.

Shadow licked his lips and smiled devilishly. Then he mouthed the words, "Do it."

Gia turned her head back to Ronnie. He'd been whining the whole time, begging for his life, and she hadn't even heard him. All she heard was the rush of her own blood in her ears. And all she felt was a hungry desire to cut through Ronnie's thick neck and split him apart.

She gritted her teeth and struck.

Her arm tore through the air, and her gill cut Ronnie diagonally from the back of his jaw all the way down to his shoulder. His skin split apart like a fine cut of aged, marbled steak. He gushed and gurgled, and Gia lavished in his every sloppy cry.

When he finally went quiet, she snatched the blonde wig right off his head, stuffing it into a bag.

Shadow hung back, wearing a sly smile and studying Gia's every move.

44

September 6th

Serena's eyes lifted open.

"Mommy?" she called out. "Mom?" Anxiety flooded through her body.

Gia wasn't there, but Togashi came to Serena's side.

Serena scanned the room and saw that she was somewhere she had never been before. And Zawade was not there with her.

"Where's Zawade?" Serena asked in a panic. "Where's Mom?"

45

September 6th

Gia clutched her bag tightly as she stepped into General Thomas's makeshift office with Awa.

General Thomas scrambled up from his desk and locked the door behind the women before he turned on them, his face twisted into an angry snarl.

"Jesus Christ!" he exploded. "When I asked you to go after Ronnie Spade, I didn't expect that you would bring an army of Arctic mermaids and slaughter half of New York. I told you to *minimize* civilian casualties. The president is beside himself."

Gia reached into her bag and pulled out a blonde wig, tossing it onto General Thomas's desk.

"I have done my part," Gia replied. "Now, will you and the president keep your word?"

He shook his head in disgust. "Of course we will." He turned his hot gaze toward Awa. "Now, you and I need to figure a way out of this mess."

Awa angled her head and glared back at the general. "Skirlor shocked me, too. I didn't expect that many soldiers to come... much less an ice kraken. Who's ever even heard of such a thing?"

"You expect me to believe that you had no prior notice that your friends from the Arctic Circle were going to attack every human in sight?"

"I had no idea!" Awa insisted, her voice rising.

The general eyed her skeptically.

Suddenly someone knocked on the door frantically. The general shooed the women to the side and cracked it open slightly.

"What is it?!" he boomed.

"Sir, it's your daughter," an aid replied, clearly in distress. "She's walking around the morgue, sir!"

* * *

GENERAL THOMAS THREW his arms around Zawade and sobbed.

"Oh, my girl... my girl. Oh, God."

She pushed him away, and a piece of her flesh flopped onto the floor.

He recoiled in horror.

A guard brought Serena into the room, and the general screamed at her, "Fix her! Fix my daughter! She's falling apart."

Gia burst into the room and ran to Serena, embracing her.

"She can't fix me, Dad!" Zawade screamed. "This is how I am now. I don't want to be here anymore. Damn it! You should have left me alone. I was good where I was!"

Tears streamed down the general's face.

"You need to let Serena go, Dad. You shouldn't be experimenting on me!"

"I'm not!" he cried. "I couldn't bear losing you."

"You have to let me rest in peace. I don't want to be here, living like this. It's not a life, Dad. I lived my life, and it ended, okay? I shouldn't be here. Necromancy is very dangerous, Dad. You don't know what you're doing."

The general cast his pleading eyes to Serena. "Help me," he sobbed.

Zawade lurched at her father and got in his face. "Listen to me! She can't do anything to help you. You have to let them leave."

The general fell to his knees.

"I'm sorry, Dad. It has to be this way."

Zawade flew across the room and placed her rotten fingers on a scalpel.

"I love you, Dad. I'll see you on the other side." Then, she stabbed herself in the temple, shoving the scalpel in and twisting it, before collapsing on the ground.

"NO!" he howled. He crawled over to her lifeless body and held it in his arms. "My baby... my girl."

Gia hooked her arms around Serena's waist and backed out of the room slowly. She wanted nothing more than to escape the insanity they were trapped in.

46

September 7th

Harper didn't expect to have her heart melt the moment she laid eyes on Serena. But it did. She felt tears welling up as Serena stepped into Langley Manor.

"You're all grown up," Harper said, her voice cracking. "I knew you were... but... I... I didn't expect this. I don't know what I expected. Come here."

Harper hugged her niece and kissed her cheek.

The rest of the crew filed in behind Serena. Awa kissed Mariama hello, and Shadow and Gia entered holding hands. Togashi was the last one through the door.

Mariama ushered everyone to the back patio. "I've got dinner set up out here."

They all took seats at the table. Harper poured wine in everyone's glasses and lifted hers for a toast. "I know things are a mess right now. But I wanted to say thank you to my friends Queen Mother Awa and Queen Consort Mariama, for giving me so much love. I couldn't have made it through the last few months without you. And to my beautiful niece, I hope to get to know you... and understand you."

Harper took a deep, deep breath before the next part. "Gia, I want you to know that I forgive you, okay? I've thought a lot about what Awa said, and I know that she's right. We are family. I hope that we can build a relationship... maybe even a friendship one day."

Shadow squeezed Gia's thigh under the table. Gia sighed and nodded at Harper, acknowledging the truce.

"Here's to friends and family," Harper said, lifting her glass above her head.

"Here, here!" Awa replied, clinking her glass against Harper's.

"Cheers, love," Shadow said, touching Gia's glass with his. He took a sip and then leaned in to kiss Gia.

The food came, and everyone dug in.

"What's next?" Harper asked Gia. "What will you do now?"

Gia gazed into Shadow's eyes and smiled at him before turning back toward Harper. "We will return to Europe."

"You and Serena?"

"Yes, and Shadow, of course." Gia wrapped her hand over his and brought it into her lap.

"I see," Harper replied, looking a bit crestfallen. "I was hoping Serena would stay a bit longer."

"I would like to," Serena said to Harper.

"Really?" Harper beamed.

"Yeah, really." Serena winced and turned her eyes to her mother's. "And also, I've been talking to Togashi, Mom... I would like to learn more about myself... about my... talents."

Gia furrowed her eyebrows. "You can do this in Monte Carlo, can you not?"

Awa leaned in. "Gia, Mariama and I will need to stay here with Harper for the foreseeable future. I have a meeting with President Bowden in a few days. I would be happy to take Serena under my wing. She's been gifted with extraordinary abilities, and I think she is destined for a greater purpose. Please allow me to teach her all I know about leadership, about courage. She will need to be strong for the challenges she will face."

Togashi nodded in agreement. "I have already ordered many texts to be brought here to me from the Archives. Had Serena been brought to us as a child, which was my wish, then perhaps we would not be where we are. I would like to teach Serena how to protect herself... and all of us."

Gia's heart thudded against her chest. She felt lightheaded at the thought of not having her girl around her. "I have barely had any time with my own daughter," Gia whispered, partly to the table and partly to herself. "My heart aches at the thought of leaving her here."

Serena pushed away from the table and came up behind her mother, putting her arms around her.

"Mommy, I love you. I can come visit you anytime. I'm going to have a lot of help here. I know that you didn't have your parents when you needed them, but I do have you. We can talk on the phone every day if you want. I have to learn to take care of myself, and Mommy, that's not something you can teach me. You developed your own ways of moving through the world, and that's not how I want to live my life. Mommy, please give me this chance."

Gia bit her lip to stop herself from crying.

"*Bene, sirenetta*," she replied finally. "I understand."

Then Gia glanced across the table leveling her eyes at Harper.

"Do not let any harm come to my daughter, Harper. Otherwise, I *will* murder you."

Harper snorted with laughter. "Oh, I *know* you will."

47

October 3rd

"Fancy a cocktail?" Shadow called out from inside Gia's yacht. The Mediterranean Sea off the coast of Monte Carlo was the color of Lapis Lazuli, and the sky was lit pink and orange by the setting sun.

Gia shouted back to him. "What is it that you silly Cockneys call a drink?"

"Ah, one of my favorite things," Shadow grinned, walking back onto the deck to face Gia. "We call that a 'tumble down the sink'."

"I will never understand you," Gia replied, taking off her sunglasses.

"That's all right, love. We have at least another... what... hundred years? You got yourself a diamond geezer now. A real high-quality merman. Give me twenty years, and you'll be chirpsin' like a Bow Bells bird."

"Queen's English, *per favore*."

"Nevermind. Now, pick your poison." He held up two liquor bottles. "We got gin and whiskey."

"Bourbon."

He chuckled. "I don't know why I asked."

Shadow dipped back into the yacht, beelining for the wet bar. He returned several minutes later, bearing a Kentucky bourbon on the rocks for Gia and a G&T for himself. He handed Gia her bevvy and then lifted his lounge chair with his free hand, setting it beside hers. He eased into his chair and reached out for Gia. Shadow took her hand in his and kissed it.

His eyes danced. "Never thought I'd have me own wife."

"*Wife*?!" Gia nearly dropped her glass.

Shadow reached into his pocket and extracted a little velvet box in the shape of a clam.

He dropped onto one knee. "Will you make me the happiest bloke in Monaco?"

He popped open the box, revealing an enormous, pear-shaped diamond, with tiny, inlaid black pearls in the band.

Stunned into silence, Gia simply laid in her chair staring at the giant rock as it glistened with the light from the sunset.

"Don't leave a brother hanging in the lurch."

"Shadow... I—"

"I know you're scared, Gia. But I ain't like those other men. *You* don't scare me. I know you don't need me to take care of you, but I'll do it anyway. We both got darkness inside, and our dark days—hell, they'll be more of 'em to come. But whatever comes, I want to face it with the biggest baddie by my side. You're my woman, Gia. The woman of my life. You're the sun to my moon. Let me light your way through the darkness."

Gia searched Shadow's eyes and found herself in them. In his soul, she saw back generations and generations—all the way to ancient times. The sea connected them, but more importantly, he had also won her trust.

She could not deny that he felt like home.

She closed her eyes.

"Vittore is going to kill me if I get married before he does. I cannot spoil his moment. He has waited a long time to marry Stavros... and I ruined the last wedding..."

Shadow stood over her, tapping his foot.

"Yes," she said, finally. "I will marry you."

He put the ring box down on the side table, rose from his chair and picked Gia up, cradling her in his arms.

"Kiss me," she commanded.

Instead, he walked over to the edge of the boat and tossed her overboard.

"Now," he shouted, "that's what you get for making me wait!"

He threw off his clothes and dove into the water as well.

Gia slipped off her bikini, and the waves carried it away.

Shadow paddled over to her and embraced her. They floated in the water together for a long while.

As the sun kissed the horizon line, Shadow tilted Gia's head toward him and grazed her lips with his. "We're gonna have adventures, babe. You and me, we're Barney Rubble."

Gia paused. "That expression... I think I remember what it means...rubble... trouble? We are... trouble?"

"See," he replied, "you're already becoming an expert in all things Mister Shadow."

Then he kissed her.

"I love you," Gia whispered. "I think you are right. I think you are *amore della mia vita...* the love of my life."

He smirked. "I'm glad you finally see that." He splashed her with his tail and then said, "I'll race you to the moon!"

He jetted off to the east, toward the rising moon. Gia rushed after him.

Their tails splashed gently in the waves—hers opal white, his silvery grey.

EPILOGUE

Queen Awa's phone buzzed. It was Moussa––again––his third call in a row. She answered this time.

"What's wrong, Moussa!? This better be an emergency." She lowered her voice and whispered. "I'm standing outside the Oval Office."

"Nothing's wrong, *Maman*! I have good news."

"Make it quick."

"Talia called to tell me that the network wants to sign us! Kyle and I are getting a reality show! They're going to film us moving our people from Brazil to California... show the blending of two colonies. The producers are very excited about having an in-depth look at merfolk in a way that's never been done before."

"Hmm," Awa replied. "I thought the plan was to stay in Brazil and raise money to rebuild in Dakar?"

"Anything we do will be easier with exposure, *Maman*. I can start a foundation and fundraise. And Kyle has promised to earmark a portion of money from his data firm to help rebuild the Coral Tower. You don't seem happy to hear this news. What's wrong, *Maman*?"

The door to the Oval Office opened, and an aide ushered Awa in.

"I have to go, son. We'll speak later."

DYING TO KNOW WHAT HAPPENS TO THE REST OF THE CHARACTERS?

Join my Insider Circle and find out.

Simply scan the QR code below and you'll receive my notoriously entertaining emails.

IF YOU LOVED THIS BOOK...

Please leave a review on Amazon!

BOOKS BY JINCEY LUMPKIN

Mermaid of Venice (Book 1)

Mermaid of Sicily (Book 2)

Mermaid of New York (Book 3)

Mermaid of Paris (Book 4)

Mermaid of St. Moritz (Book 5)

Mermaid of Monte Carlo (Book 6)

Sirena de Venecia (*Mermaid of Venice*, the Spanish language version)

A SPECIAL SNEAK PEEK
AT LITTLE HOUSE BY THE BRIDGE

I.

The Midnight Whisper

A freight train passed under the rickety bridge in front of the house, and a wall of noisy air blasted past the front porch. I couldn't sleep. The rednecks across the way were hooting and hollering again, playing their twangy music.

I took a swig of bourbon and tossed a klonopin to the back of my throat, see-sawing in the rocking chair, waiting to feel woozy. The whole town was louder and slower than I remembered. It was a wonder that my mother could close her eyes and block out the noise to sleep.

The street lamp flickered as something rustled in the patch of woods next to our little house. I glared into the darkness and imagined a pair of black eyes staring back. A terrible thought.

After that, I really did feel as if there was something awful looking at me. The street light blinked off, and it scared me so much that I shot up and went inside, locking the bolt behind me.

As I made my way through the house, I traveled through my

memories. How, for example, there had been a time where I'd tied a rubber band around the crystal knobs of the French doors leading from the dining room into my bedroom. All I had craved was a little privacy, but my parents had to walk through my room to get to theirs. So, during the year and a half when we'd lived in that tiny, somewhat Victorian house, I hadn't been offered much in the way of alone time.

The In-Between-House, we called that place. I had my own name for it: the Little House by the Bridge.

It was the house we stayed after we sold our place on the cul-de-sac, but while we were still in the process of building our big, peach-colored house at the Club.

I remembered sitting in my mom's lap in the kitchen when I was seven, watching her open the Sunday paper and find that my Mother's Day poem I'd written about her and discovering that it had won first place. The prize was a $100 savings bond at the local bank.

I thought about dinnertime and lima beans and dipping my hands into the deep sink filled with soapy water, as I helped my dad clean up.

I found my way into my old room and laid down, my head filling with warm waves as the meds kicked in.

And just as I started to head into oblivion, I heard a whisper.

"Violet..."

It was a man's voice, soft and deep. My heart knocked so loudly against the wall of my chest that I felt my pulse sear into my eyeballs. Immediately, my eyelids stretched open as wide as they could go, and I focused on the ceiling. I dared not look in the shadows.

He whispered again, this time nearer to my face.

"Meet me in the woods."

* * *

2.

The Anxious Gravestone

The smell of bacon coupled with the warm, doughy sweetness of buttermilk biscuits roused me from the bed and brought me to consciousness.

How long had I laid in the dark last night, waiting vigilantly for another phantom whisper?

I felt as if I was a child all over again. I had longed to wake my mother and tell her what I heard as well as what I imagined I saw in the woods, but I had resisted.

Adults were strong and pragmatic, and I needed to face whatever came my way. Regardless, one day soon my mother wouldn't be there to shield me from the figures lurking in the shadows—or from more mundane threats, like hurt feelings and failures. No, it was time to grow up, to be grown, and so I'd laid alone in my room half the night resisting the darkness around me.

In daylight, almost anything feels surmountable, especially after a hot, buttered biscuit.

"Morning, Violet," my mother said. "Set the table for me?"

I glanced down. "You must be feeling better today, judging by this spread."

"The doctor says I should cook whatever sparks my appetite."

My mom loved place settings. My aunt once told me that my mom, at age thirteen, had slammed a pitchfork into the heavy dirt at her family's farm and said, "One day, I swear, I'm not gonna be having to do all this!"

She always said the stork had dropped her off at the wrong house. Her life, she had determined, would be in the city, and it would be fancy. She only got half of what she wanted.

Sterling silver forks, knives and spoons, Blue Danube china, cotton linens with an abstract sunflower print on a grass-green background—I laid all these familiar things carefully on the butcher block table and proceeded to pour myself a glass of water.

My mother was pulling crumpled strips of bacon from the cast-iron skillet.

I watched her hands, her dainty wrists.

She was an old woman now, with age spots and translucent skin that offered a glimpse of blue veins that twisted and turned like the lines on a subway map.

Of course, it made sense that she was older. I, myself, was well into my thirties.

Nonetheless, it surprised me to see her frail, witness her moving slowly—from what I knew of my mother, she seemed incapable of slowness. After all, in her prime, the woman had ripped up the interstate between Oak Mill and Atlanta. Countless sets of tires met their demise thanks to her lead foot. She was a force who commanded every room, demanded attention. The spotlight had never failed to find her.

But now, she had become a soft and distant echo of herself. It seemed that a light had dimmed, and was getting ready to be flipped off completely.

Or maybe this was always who she had been, and I'd only seen her larger-than-life because I was so small, viewing her through a proverbial magnifying lens.

***

After breakfast, I got in my car and drove without a destination. I passed the courthouse, where I recalled the time when my father once had a client lie down in the middle of the courtroom to demonstrate how badly the guy's back was spasming after a trucking accident. He was rather theatrical, my Dad, and I smiled at the recollection. I meandered up onto Pine Mountain and through the campus of my old school, which had long since been abandoned.

The school had been relocated for some mysterious reason. One summer day, a team in hazmat suits erected a fence, and closed the whole campus. Now, the city had a dream about making the site a public park.

As I rounded the drive, I saw that the road to the big house had been covered up, as if the woods and green and kudzu had reclaimed it. Nature had been so aggressive in its take back of its property that I couldn't even see a structure in the distance. Later, I drove on the small highway to look for the gate that had allowed entry at one point in time, but I couldn't locate it.

Strange.

It was like someone had erased its existence completely. And along with it, severed my memories, as though they were never really real.

Never saw kids drinking coke on the sofas in the lounge.

Never learned French from a real French lady.

Never played Oregon Trail in the computer lab.

Never avoided the hot dragon breath of the librarian who was never seen eating food.

A chill ran over me. The place radiated bad energy. And I sped away, dazed.

The town was quite woodsy—Georgia Pines and Oak and Pecan trees. It was high spring, and everything was overly green, showing off. Every bush was blooming, every tree was fully unleashed. The air vibrated with extra oxygen. One could almost get the idea that this was a healthy place, a place for life. However, I could see beyond the illusion and felt the deep darkness of this place. Hundreds of years of brutality and muffled screams.

I stopped by the graveyard off Mississippi Street to visit my father. The large white monument was marbling elegantly as the years passed. And there, on the obelisk, his beautiful poem.

> *YOUTH*
> *Let us live in a lull*
> *of the long winter-winds,*
> *where the shy*
> *silver-antlered reindeer go,*
> *on dainty hoofs*
> *with their white rabbit friends,*
> *amidst the delicate flowering snow.*
> *All of our thoughts*
> *will be fairer than doves.*
> *We will live upon wedding cake*
> *frosted with sleet.*
> *We will build us a house*

from two red tablecloths,
And wear scarlet mittens
on both hands and feet.
Let us live in a land
of whispering trees,
alder and aspen
and poplar and birch.
Singing out prayers
in a pale sea-green breeze,
with star-flower rosaries
and moss banks for church
All of our dreams
will be clearer than glass,
clad in the water
and sun as you wish.
We will watch the white feet
of young morning pass
and dine upon honey
and small shiny fish.
—Henry Monroe Carroll, Jr.

I lingered in the fresh-cut grass for some time, staring at the monument. Reading and re-reading the poem. I thought about how, in that last year of his life, I'd inspired my father to write. He rediscovered poetry and read me things he enjoyed, things he found meaning in. He jotted stanzas down throughout the day, between clients, like a kind of legal-eagle William Carlos Williams. He would hand me scribbled notes, which I'd edit. We quibbled frequently over line breaks. I was in college then, and neither of us knew that in ten years I'd be a writer—and in three months he'd be dead.

Here's what nobody tells you about grief: It never goes away. Yeah, of course you accept it after a fashion. They're gone. They're not coming back. It's all perfectly logical, but it will never make sense. I found out that he'd died from a family friend who had called me.

"I'm so sorry about your dad," he said.

As far as I knew, my dad was in the hospital, but I didn't know for what. A heart attack was my guess. No one was telling me anything, they all refused to share their knowledge, and I couldn't get a hold of my mom.

"I'm just so sorry, Violet. Please tell me where the funeral is, so I can send flowers."

Funeral?

I hung up the phone and screamed in the middle of some empty parking garage. I was twenty-one then, and I hardly knew anything about the world, but I realized in that moment I'd have to grow up–– and grow up fast.

My mind wandered slowly back to the present and I transfered to my gaze to my mom's gravestone. Carved already into the stone was her name, her birthday, a dash and then... nothing.

The blank space reminded me of a computer cursor––how it blinks aggressively until you satisfy it with letters and numbers. It eagerly willed her death simply to fill in the blank, to complete the thought, to finish its job.

Farther down in the family plot were empty spaces, other graves. There was even one marked with my name on the headstone.

And as much as I wanted to, I could not look away from what would become my eternal resting place. The grass swayed as a breeze drifted over my shoulders, bidding me welcome, as if the lush greenery and the dirt beneath me were calling for me to enter.

I was overcome with that same sensation I'd felt the previous night: hot eyes on me, the feeling of being closely observed.

But I was all alone in the cemetery, and there was not another living soul in sight.

* * *

3.

Secrets in the Basement

Dust made angry dragon tails in the air as I sifted through over twenty-five years of my father's client files. I wore a mask, goggles, and gloves at the insistence of my mother. It was a good idea, really, since the files were musty and warped with mildew from a flood that had occurred years ago.

I had volunteered to clean out my father's old office, in anticipation of the real estate closing. Our family had snapped up all kinds of property, and many years before, Dad had moved his legal office into the home where he grew up. As we sold our buildings off one at a time, it felt like we were ripping off little pieces of our history and throwing them in the shredder.

But that's what one does; one moves forward.

I started in the basement, deciding to do the messiest job first, believing I would have something to look forward to once I reached sorting the inside of the house. Some file cabinets in the basement were rusted shut and needed to be hauled off by professionals. As for everything else, I would have to comb through it myself.

My mom felt there might be sensitive and private information in the files. She sure was right about that.

As I opened banker boxes labeled by year, I was surprised to see that even some of my friends had been to see my father to solve their legal woes. In the files I found various misdemeanors, traffic tickets, and even one rape. My father had never breathed a word of any of this to me. He'd kept everyone's secrets.

I noticed the name of one ex-boyfriend labeled on a file, and I peeked inside. The boy had been charged with a felony for marijuana possession with intent to sell.

Case Status: Dismissed.

How interesting. I had gone to a school dance with that boy around the time of the alleged crime on file. It suddenly made sense why Dad was very unhappy about me seeing that boy. My father had handled things very smoothly, though, and hadn't pressured me to stop seeing the boy. In fact, I broke things off on my own accord, after he got particularly rough with me while we were kissing one night.

I put that file to the side to save it, along with the other incriminating ones about folks I knew. I then dumped a big stack of boring files into a heavy-duty black trash bag. What a mess.

After hauling the first load of trash to the dump and driving home, I zipped the contraband files into freezer bags and slid them under my bed.

As I threw my clothes into the washer and hopped into the shower, I fantasized about what other treasures might await me in the basement of my father's office. Now that I'd discovered a goldmine of information on the townspeople, my so-called former neighbors, the whole town seemed to sizzle with promise.

Was this why Dad had stayed so long in the little town where he grew up? My father, the one-time mayor, must have liked being the keeper of secrets. He must have basked in the influence he had held, the knowledge he possessed. He would have been able to wield extraordinary power. Had he weaponized the town secrets?

One way or another, something told me that keeping the files would come in handy

I stepped out of the shower and walked into my room, which felt unseasonably cold, as if I had just walked through a door an into a freezer. I caught a sudden chill and my heart jumped abruptly.

Again, I had the sense I was not alone.

Thank you very much, I won't be needing any ghost visits tonight.

And with that, I took off like the Road Runner into my mother's room.

"Can I sleep in here tonight?" I begged.

For God's sake, I was reverting to a child, but honestly, I didn't care. I preferred a little embarrassment over the prospect of once again trying to close my eyes and pretend everything was normal, as some demonic creature stared at me from the corner.

* * *

4.

Hiding in the Pines

"Do you remember when we thought we lost you?" My mom asked as I lay beside her in bed, during a commercial break for *House Hunters International*. "You had asked to sleep in the bed, and I told you no. Then I fell asleep. I woke up with a bad feeling."

The story felt vaguely familiar, but was not fully accessible as I searched my memory.

My mom continued without my acknowledgement or denial. "Well, I asked your daddy where you were, and he went to your room, and you weren't there. We searched all over. Called your name a thousand times. A child molester client of your father's lived in the shack across the way, and your dad became convinced that the man taken you. He was so torn up about it that he threw up. We called the police, and they searched all over at the rednecks' place, but to no avail. Finally, your sister sat down on a pile of laundry that was on the couch here in the bedroom and woke you up. You'd burrowed down into the dirty clothes. I felt terrible and promised myself I'd never again turn you away from my bed."

It seemed comical to me that I was such a heavy sleeper back then. Of course, all of that would change in a few years when I eventually began suffering from severe insomnia. Sometimes at night I would see a shimmering, opalescent light hovering over the closed door in my bedroom.

A spirit? An angel?

It was unsettling, sure, but didn't seem bad. I didn't get any ominous feelings from it, no bad vibrations.

However, I never told anyone either, except one friend who also saw it during a sleepover. We examined it from all angles to determine if it was some trick of the light, but it surely wasn't. It was something unexplainable.

When Mom and I finally turned off the television, I dreamt of my father. He was in the back office, seated at his big mahogany desk. On it was a bronze sculpture his father had made: two men in a boxing ring, a tiny thing, maybe 3 inches wide. He barely noticed me as I stood across from him. I felt anxious and desperate.

"Where have you been?" I demanded.

He glanced up from a thick stack of files, annoyed, "Right here," he said.

I was confused. I knew he'd been gone for quite a long time, but I didn't realize it had been over fifteen years.

"Have you been working the whole time?" I asked, my eyes starting to water.

"Well, someone has to," he snapped. I felt I was shrinking. The desk appeared higher and the wing-chairs taller. I backed away.

Before I reached the door he peered down at me and said, "While you're here, why don't you put back those files you took?"

As I walked through the house, it began to spring to life. Secretaries pounded away on typewriters in the dining room. A man exited the bathroom through its frosted glass door. I walked through the waiting room, and every face stared at me, hotly. I was burning with shame and felt in danger.

A little boy and girl who were seated on the porch swing stopped their playing to glare at me as I walked out the front door.

"You're a sinner," the boy said, his voice full of scorn. "It's obvious."

I woke up shivering, drenched in sweat. My mom was lying beside me, snoring in the soft, high-pitched way she did, and I felt anxious. I checked my phone, and it was thirteen minutes past two o'clock in the morning. I saw a movie once that said three o'clock in the morning is the true witching hour, so waking up just before three was poor indicator for getting back to sleep.

So instead of even trying to reenter a sleep state, I read the news on my phone. Nothing of note. The minutes ticked on; fifteen, twenty, thirty minutes passed. Finally, around seven minutes before three o'clock, I decided to get up and face whatever might be coming for me, head-on.

I tried my best to not think about scary movie previews where paranormal entities possessed the power to string people up by their ankles and such. I decided that a hoodie might help me feel more courageous, like a protective shield, so I grabbed one hanging off a chair in the dining room and zipped it closed over me.

A flash of light reflected against the porch window.

I jumped.

Then I realized my hoodie's zipper had caught the light.

I couldn't decide if being inside or outside was more terrifying. I finally settled on outside, because I imagined that if anything in the house were to attack me, I would have had to run outside anyway. Plus, I could sprint across the street to the rednecks' house and pound on their door if I truly needed to find safety.

So, I unbolted the lock and sat down in the rocking chair, just as I had the night before.

This proved to be really bad idea.

At first, all I could see was the moon and an empty street, and beyond that, the cold metal of the railroad tracks. I curled my legs into the rocking chair and swayed a little. How, in one solitary day, could the noise of the town go silent? You could have heard a rat pee on a piece of cotton.

There wasn't even any wind.

I stared down the lane to the revamped Depot, red at the edge of the tracks. The town still used old bulbs, and they glowed in a goldish hue, which was a comfort on such a lonely night. I thought of my new home, back in New York, and I imagined the activity that would be happening at that late hour, like bodega cats rustling between shelves of cereal, late night revelers emptying out of bars, and people riding to and from the airport. But here? Everyone in the goddamn town was asleep except for me.

Then, in the distance, my eyes caught movement.

Past the train depot was an old house that had been converted into a nursing home. On the front lawn of the home was a dollhouse replica of of the big house. The small white door on the front of the dollhouse slammed shut, with an outsized sound for something so small.

I examined at the miniature house, with its Ionic columns, and strained my eyes to see what might be inside.

Suddenly my attention was pulled away from the nursing home's front yard. There was a sound behind my house, like sticks breaking. It sounded close. I lost my breath.

I wanted to see what caused the noise. But I also didn't... I dreaded the truth.

In the woods to my right, there was a glint of something. A highlight, subtle, but perceptible. Otherworldly.

I felt like I was being watched again. And it was the worst feeling, made my mouth go dry and reduced my feet to pins and needles.

In the distance, by the nursing home, something light-colored, like a small piece of fabric floated across the yard, and whatever lurked in the woods near my house took a step backward. I heard the crunch of old pine needles.

Was the thing receding or considering its next move?

I surely was not going to wait to find out.

I bolted from the chair and flew into the house, directly to my mother's bedside, shaking her awake.

I gasped, feeling the words strangled in my throat.

"Something... something's in the woods, Mom. Please, wake up."

And as if on command, she shot straight up.

* * *

5.

Mother-Daughter Mission

"What, what are you saying?" My mother blurted out, half screaming.

"I saw something out there in the woods."

Her feet were dangling off the bed as she tried to fully wake herself up and figure out what to do. "Did you see who it was?"

I shook my head. "Not who, Mom! It was a *what*."

"Tell me *exactly* what you saw!" Her voice was angry from fear.

I stood sideways, to be able to speak to her and to keep an eye on the window facing front yard. "Tonight, it was... there was a reflection or something, and... a noise... but last night—"

She interrupted me by inhaling loudly, both from shock and from trying to catch her breath. "You saw something last night? Why didn't you tell me?"

Her eyes shone with glassy panic.

Why hadn't I told her?

Maybe because she was overly superstitious. Or maybe it was because I somehow wanted to feel special. There was something beguiling about being haunted. It made me feel like the lead in a horror film.

"I don't know, Mom...."

She shook her head from side to side, almost jerking it. "You must tell me these things, Violet! You have to inform me about any abnormal occurrences like this! I keep track, you know."

"You keep track?" I yelped. "Does this happen a lot?"

She ignored my questions. "Go get the flashlight from the drawer in the kitchen. We're going into the woods."

A mission. That's what my mother called any "investigative" work she might undertake. In another life she could have been head of the F.B.I., or at minimum a private detective.

In college we had carried out an important mother-daughter mission: spying on a boyfriend I suspected of cheating.

She drove me across state lines and rented a car at the airport. We bought wigs.

She had packed two sets of binoculars, and we staked out my boyfriend's apartment from the church parking lot across the street.

She instructed me to call him every hour in order to verify his whereabouts. While we discovered that he did lie to me, we were ultimately unsuccessful in our mission to collect evidence of his infidelity.

However in the woods next to the Little House by the Bridge, we set out on an entirely different kind of mission. One that iced my pulse so much I thought I might stop breathing.

Mom led the way, carrying the flashlight.

She held onto my arm as we walked through the pine trees. "Slower," she said, "I'm not steady on my feet anymore."

My heart beat fast, but I also felt safer being with her, confronting this thing... this ghost or demon or whatever it was.

"Where did you see it?" she asked.

"Not sure... maybe near the edge of the trees, by the road?"

The small strip of pines separated our house from my father's office and his family's former diner.

Twigs broke as we went. The fresh smell of sap and Spring filled the air.

The light bounced off branches making long shadows on the ground.

And then, by the pointed outer rim of the forest, we saw something.

It appeared to be a pile of trash and sticks and pinecones and bits of paper and hair and an unidentifiable furry substance. The collection of mush resembled a hairball or a poorly digested squirrel snack, except it was the size of a campfire.

"What in the Sam Hill is *this*?" my mother whispered. "Flash the light down there."

We crouched by the pile.

"Take a sample," she ordered.

I let out a soft cry. "No way! Not touching that stuff."

She shoved me out of the way and dug her hand into the mess. "It's wet," she said, "sticky."

In the blue glow of the flashlight, I could see that the wad she was holding had shredded paper in it. On the paper, printed words.

"This looks like the start of a bird's nest," I said.

"No," my mom clicked her tongue, "this is a warning."

WANT TO KNOW WHAT HAPPENS NEXT? JOIN MY FREE MEMBERS' AREA AT JINCEYLUMPKIN.COM/MEMBERS